Graves Robbed, Heirlooms Returned

Reed Lavender: 1

Ashley Capes

For Brooke

Chapter 1.

In the bright moonlight, Reed Lavender inserted his best crowbar into the pine box where the top met the sides and wrenched the steel down. Wood squeaked and he shuddered. *Worse than fingernails on a blackboard.* He lifted the lid free, resting it against the freshly turned earth – which, unlike the sound of an opening coffin – was an almost pleasant thing. A pungent scent, but real. Honest. Worms and bugs, minerals and secrets lived in the earth; when you got right down to it, grave dirt wasn't really any different to regular dirt.

And he was certainly down to it now, about to be elbow-deep in a coffin.

Again.

But for what they'd given Elise, the word 'coffin' was a stretch. A pine box wasn't much of a final resting place – dignity hardly came cheap in Rikerton's funeral home and unclaimed bodies were lucky to avoid the incinerator. Or maybe that would have been better. *Dust to dust and all that.*

"But then you'd be out of work," he told himself.

Elise the runaway – that's what the police thought she was – lay in her dirty jeans and the same faded Pink Floyd t-shirt she wore when she walked into the cafe two days back. Her arms lay at her sides, cuts on her palms mostly hidden. Her face had been covered... by a used napkin. "Jesus, Jennings, that the best you could do?" Reed growled. At least the napkin was in one piece; the undertaker had been known to be far more slipshod at times.

Reed lifted the napkin... and ground his teeth.

She'd been beaten blue. Deep bruises swam across her cheeks, one eye swollen shut and the other just as blackened, torn skin at her temple. Jennings had cleaned her face up well enough but there were still leaf fragments and dried blood in her hair. The pallor of death had washed out Elise's freckles, mere suggestions crossing her bent nose. *God, what is she, fifteen? She looks so small.*

Reed tossed the napkin aside and unwound his scarf, folded it and placed it over her face, standing still a moment, shaking as he blinked. The night air ran chill fingers across his now-exposed throat and the back of his neck. Finally, he took a breath and leant over the coffin, where he lifted her arm. "Sorry, sweetheart," he said softly, twisting her silver bracelet up to the moon. Only the letters 'Elise' engraved there. Really, there was little he could learn from a perfunctory glance at her clothing and jewellery that the police wouldn't have already catalogued. He'd check that later, of course – but Elise deserved more.

No, he'd have to wake her up – sort of.

Her last words would maybe be enough of a clue. Most folks didn't have much to say, right before the end. Sometimes it was a scream or a grunt if he was unlucky. Other times, they addressed their killer. Or a loved one, perhaps, if the death was peaceful. *Not that I've heard a lot of those in my time.*

There'd been a man out west, he couldn't recall where - so many cities and towns blended together - whose last words had been an apology for burnt toast. After that, the poor guy hadn't said a thing before being t-boned at an intersection by a bus an hour later, two blocks from his office.

But sometimes, a person's last sentence held a clue.

"Come on, Elise, tell me something I can use."

If she didn't, he had no other supernatural tricks up his sleeve either, since he couldn't simply call upon her spirit. It would have made things much easier *and* allowed him to stop violating peoples' graves but sadly, he wasn't that lucky.

Reed removed the scarf a moment, took her cold hands and closed his eyes, sending his awareness down through her mute fingertips, pushing his way along quiet veins until he reached her chest, still echoing with the memory of a million heartbeats, then at last up the throat to the tongue; the tongue which remembered everything.

But it would move only once more.

"In the name of Mors, speak any that you might," he whispered. "I'll help you if you can."

Her body resisted.

Not unusual. It meant reliving the pain and shock – why wouldn't her body want to fight that? It was at rest now, if not at peace. But he had to know. Reed pushed harder, pouring both his hope and anger into the request. "Please, Elise."

A flicker, a tiny sound as her jaw shifted.

He opened his eyes and leant close. Would it be a scream? A clue? Nonsense? Her voice was little more than a rasping whisper, such as might easily be mistaken for a breeze, but he caught the words.

"Wow, what a beautiful view. This is some place; you can see half the city from here."

Then silence.

"Shit." Poor girl, she probably never saw it coming.

Reed lowered Elise's hands. *Half the city.* That hardly narrowed things down – there were only *hundreds* of such high points available. But it probably put the owner in a certain tax bracket at least. He shook his head. *No assumptions.* It was his first rule. And that went for murder too – maybe it was an accident. Still, *something* happened to bring Elise's life to an unjust end.

He had to find out; no-one else was looking and Elise's grandmother deserved answers. Even unpleasant ones, he supposed.

Reed placed the scarf back over the girl's face and reached for his shovel.

Chapter 2.

A buzz-saw was grinding its way into his skull – then out through the other side and into the wall. Or so it seemed.

Steve. Had to be.

"Again? Damn it." Reed rolled over in bed, throwing the heavy blankets aside and groaning when his feet hit cold floorboards. In the dimness, he fumbled the curtains open, squinting against the new light. Cold air prickled his skin as he gripped the window sill, fighting off the rush of blood that assaulted his head. *Stupid. Shouldn't have got up so fast.*

Beyond the frosted glass the cul-de-sac between apartments was empty – but across the way, one of his neighbours, Steve, stood in the gaping wall-cavity dressed in a heavy jacket, woollen hat and earmuffs, shearing through timber spread across two A-frames. An orange extension cord ran back across the floor, lost in all manner of serious-looking renovation equipment.

Reed opened the window and stuck his head into the winter air. "Steve!" he shouted.

The man didn't look up.

Reed sighed. *You're wasting your time, bonehead.* He slammed the window and strode into his dim living room. There, he snatched his grey coat off the hook, grabbed his keys and jammed both feet into his Cons, still dirty from last night's trip to the cemetery.

In the silvery elevator, Reed folded his arms as it lurched its way down.

Management had put up a poster, urging residents of the Grand Towers to avoid sending bags of unattended rubbish down to the lobby. One of the joys of having intermittent cameras.

After far, far too long, he crossed the lobby, nodding to which ever uniformed chap was on reception, and shoved his way through the glass doors. Outside, the dishevelled garden lay empty but he still nearly tripped on uneven paving stones as he headed to the other side of the apartment building and pressed for the elevator.

Fifth floor.

Around the corner, down the scuffed, navy blue carpet and into number twenty – unlocked of course. The roar of the circular saw filled a cluttered room, rushing through workbenches, stacks of lumber and paint and even the odd support column.

Reed charged toward his neighbour.

"Hey!"

Steve turned, cut the saw and gave a wide grin as he removed his ear muffs. His green eyes twinkled above an unshaven face. "Morning, Reed. No pants today, huh?"

"Forget about that, it's seven *am*," Reed said. "And I'm wearing boxers under the coat, all right?"

"Sure. So, how can I help?"

Reed drew in a breath. "It's a bit early for the saw, isn't it? I didn't exactly get a lot of sleep last night." After laying Elise back to rest, he stumbled back to his dented Ford Falcon and drove home as the moon waned, no closer to a lead.

On the way into the lobby, he'd glanced up to the tiny raven symbol he'd scratched above the glass doors – all was well – then dragged himself inside, up and into the shower.

A glass of milk followed and then bed.

And that was probably only... what, four hours ago? His limbs still weighed ten times their usual amount and the cold wasn't helping; it was like a million tiny bites from invisible icicles on any piece of exposed skin.

"Sorry, but I have to finish these renovations," Steve said. "You know how it is."

"You live alone, Steve – no-one's on your back about them."

Steve raised his hands. "Hey, I'm the most popular guy in the building. Guys love this sort of thing; they help me half the time, just to feel useful."

"Yeah?" Reed glanced around.

Empty.

Yet, no-one's here complaining, either.

"Come on, once I'm done I'll invite you over for the greatest party the Grand Towers – nah, the *city* – has ever seen."

Reed sighed. "Fine, how about tomorrow you start at nine, instead?"

"Yeah, no problems."

"Thanks." Reed started back toward his distant bed.

"Oh, there was something. You had a visitor last night;

caught her at reception."

Reed turned. Probably Elise's grandmother, Irene. "An old lady with a cane?"

"No, younger than that. She said for you to call her, said her name was Mona." Steve scratched his head. "You know, now that I think of it – I can't really remember what she looks like, isn't that funny?"

"It was definitely Mona?" he asked, missing half a step.

"Yep."

"Right then, I'll give her a call," Reed said and headed outside and then back to his apartment, where he slumped into a creaking armchair.

Mona – the name Aunty Mors used when she crossed the Fringe and dropped in on the humans. *Mors* in the old roman. *Thanatos* in ancient Greek – *Death* in regular, plain old English. *Whatever she wants, it's not going to be good news.*

But he'd have to call her later.

Today he had to meet with Irene and figure out his next move. Maybe one more visit to the police, see what they had.

Or the cafe first, he could meet Irene there.

"Done." Reed pushed himself out of the chair and dialled the *Delion Cafe* – close enough to Flinders Street Station that she wouldn't have too far to walk but that the meal would still be decent.

***

Elvis Costello's *Everyday I Write the Book* sent its

upbeat pop from the speakers outside the *Delion Cafe*, a yellow warmth from the windows, people removing coats and taking to the deep green vinyl seats with expectant expressions.

His own face was probably a mirror when he entered, struck by heat and the sizzle of bacon. *Eggs too, man that smells good. Maybe eggs Benedict today?* Reed almost snorted. Only if Irene could pay him, and he had a suspicion she'd spent enough on the train, not to mention two nights in the city so far – not easy on a pensioner's budget.

She waved him over to a seat in the back with an anxious smile.

"I have a little news," he said as he sat.

"Oh, thank you, Mr Lavender." Irene took a sip from the black coffee before her. Her white hair was tied into a bun, same as before, but her make-up was less diligently applied today. "What can you tell me about Elise? And the bracelet?"

He drew it from a pocket coat and passed the bracelet across the table. Irene's hand trembled as she took the silver, but she squeezed her fingers over it as she thanked him. "I gave this to her mother, you know... when she was Elise's age and her mother gave it to Elise. You've done a good thing, even if it was a sin."

"Well..."

"And why those dipsticks wouldn't pay to have her exhumed, I'll never understand. It's bad enough that I'm only told about their idiocy *after* she's been buried. What kind of funeral home is Rickerton even running?"

Sara the waitress arrived, pad in hand. Her apron bore the *Delion* logo – leaves swirling. She gave him a quick smile – he was regular enough to warrant that – then looked to Irene. "Can I get you some breakfast?"

"Nothing for me, dear," Irene said.

"Chocolate milkshake please," Reed said. That was more within his price range.

Sara chuckled. "Sure thing."

Irene gave him a look. "Aren't you too old to be ordering something like that?"

"I guess I just don't like the idea of getting old – no offense, of course."

She waved a hand. "Not to worry. So, what did you want to tell me?"

Here was the tricky part. He didn't know anything really, but in addition to the bracelet, he had to give her some hope. And reassurance. "I have a clue but I haven't followed it up, I need help first so I'm going to the police again."

"Hope they do more for you than they offered me," she said, taking a sip of her coffee, seemingly satisfied.

"In the meantime, did you by chance remember anything about why she might have come here from Nowa Nowa? It's a fair hike."

Irene sighed. "Still no idea, Mr Lavender. I don't think she even knew anyone here. Who knows, with the internet? Maybe it was drugs after all – she was a bright girl but she was always going to this or that party." She shrugged then. "Same as me when I was her age, I guess."

Getting a hold of Elise's computer might have been helpful but that wasn't likely. Reed spread his hands. "Seems a long way to travel to score something."

"That's what I thought." Irene pushed herself up from the table, one hand reaching for her cane. "Well, I'd better let you get back to work. You know where to reach me; and thank you for the bracelet, Mr Lavender."

He nodded.

Sara soon arrived with his milkshake. He accepted it with a smile. "Sara, can I ask you a question or two?"

She flicked a stray wisp of hair back. "Sure, just be quick, okay?"

He took a straw, started his milkshake and nodded to himself. Not too sweet. "I'll be quick. It's about Elise again."

Sara's expression fell a little. "No good news?"

"Not really. Tell me again, what did she do?"

Sara shrugged. "You sound like a cop, Reed."

"Well, private investigators sound like cops for a reason, you know."

"Yeah." Sara said. "You could just read the police report."

"I suppose, but I can't ask it follow-up questions."

"Clever. Well, she came in the morning, looking real cold, and ordered a coffee. She sat by herself, near the window – I forget which table. She looked outside every now and then, as if she was waiting for someone but no-one showed."

"Did she have a computer with her?"

"Like I said before, she had nothing. She drank her coffee and left without paying. She never said a word to anyone but me, to order. I thought she was a little bitch for running out on her bill... but then when they found her... I felt like shit for thinking it."

"Don't be too hard on yourself," Reed said. "Anything else?"

"She had a nice voice, like, when she hummed to herself. That's it," Sara said with a smile. "I better get back to it."

"Right. Thanks." He took another long drink from the

milkshake. Elise hadn't seemed scared enough to want to hide out – the cafe was a public place in the heart of the city, yet she didn't have any money either. And she was over 350 kilometres from home.

And she had a nice voice, apparently – that much was new but it wasn't much to go on. *Which leaves Duong at the station – if he's not in one of his moods.* Reed finished his milkshake, paid and headed for the car. *Time to find out.*

Chapter 3.

Detective Duong leant back in his chair as he exhaled a thin trail of smoke, which slowly climbed to the water-stained ceiling of the station. The walls were a muted, dark blue – as if signalling the profession of those within. The man's boots rested on the edge of his desk and he ran a hand through his dark hair, a wavy mess. "No way."

Reed raised his hands. "Look, I really will fix you up; it'll just take a while."

"I won't need a car when I'm ninety."

"Fair point," Reed said with a grin. "In the meantime, let me owe you another favour. I just need a summary, not the whole report. What do you guys know?"

Duong jammed his cigarette into the ashtray on his desk; uneven edges gave it the look of a high school arts and crafts project. "A big favour, Lavender."

"Deal."

"Fine." He rolled back to a filing cabinet and rummaged about, before drawing a file out. Then he slid back to the desk, scratching at his beard. "So. Elise Roberts, sixteen.

Resident of Nowa Nowa in the far east, reported missing a week ago and found in the nature reserve behind the Bay City golf course two days later. No evidence of sexual assault or drugs in her system."

"So there was an autopsy?"

"Yeah. No formal ID until her grandmother arrived; the only identifying item found on her was a silver bracelet."

"Odd that the killer left it behind, don't you think?"

Duong shrugged. "Who says the killer knew what they were doing? Probably some junkie who took her bag and, when it didn't go as planned, killed and dumped her."

"They still tried to hide her body."

"Not well enough," Duong said. His eyes skimmed ahead. "Not much else here. She was seen at Flemington Station where she tried to busk, presumably for fare, and that was the last anybody saw her. Six o clock in the evening."

Reed straightened. "Where to?"

"No-one we interviewed knew."

"The ticket stand?"

Duong shut the file and tossed it onto the desk with a smile. "What does 'no-one' mean to you?"

"Then you won't mind if I visit them anyway?"

"I do mind but I don't care to stop you either, so get going already."

Reed thanked him and started for the door with a little bit of a spring in his step. A picture was forming. *Young girl uses all her money to cross the state, waits in a cafe for a meeting. When no-one shows, she heads to the station to try and get out of the city?*

"About that favour, Lavender."

He turned. "Yeah?"

"I'll be expecting it soon."

"So long as it doesn't spoil what's left of my reputation," he said with a grin.

Duong chuckled. "Think even that's worth protecting?"

"Doubt I'd get out of bed if I didn't."

Outside, he skipped across the footpath, eliciting a grumble from a woman in a suit, then twisted again to avoid a man walking his Labrador, then leapt across the street to catch a tram that was rattling its way toward the stop; a line of faces waited above heavy jackets and coats.

By the time he reached his Falcon, settling into the seat with a grunt, he'd decided Bay City golf course would be getting a visit too.

A hand fell across his shoulder. "Hello, cousin."

Reed flinched, then groaned – ignoring laughter from the back seat. He twisted around to find a pale man dressed in dark leathers, a pink scarf at his throat and aviator sunglasses covering his eyes.

"Max," Reed said with a sigh. Maximilian, one of Death's twenty offspring, and – technically – his cousin. Reed hadn't met them all yet; some didn't care for his lifestyle, it seemed. Or maybe they were simply busy with the endless harvest and shepherding that was the family business. Lotta people died every day. Maybe something like 150,000 per day and Aunty didn't oversee each one. "What do you want?"

"Lovely greeting, Reed," Max said. "Mother says you're ignoring her so I'm here to remind you to call her."

"I haven't forgotten. Is something wrong?"

"She won't say – just don't forget."

"That's not likely," he said, reaching into the console for

a jar of ribbon-striped mints. "So how come you're acting as messenger boy? And why are you dressed like a vampire from the set of *Grease*?"

"Hilarious, cousin. And vampires don't come to Melbourne anymore, everyone knows that." He shrugged. "I'm helping because I'm working in the area is all."

Reed popped one of the mints into his mouth. "Anyone I know?"

"It's always possible – how many residents of Green Hills Nursing Home are you on a first name basis with?"

"Ah."

"Well, off I go. And be a good nephew, call your aunty."

Reed opened his mouth to reply but Max was already gone. Between blinks, he'd disappeared, as was his style. The scent of olive oil lingered. Reed wound the window down and started the car. Maybe the wind would blow out the memories too – olives always put him in the mind of his parents.

Hardly happy memories, right?

By the time he reached the Flemington Station – halfway across the damn city – he was sweating. He hummed along to Soundgarden on the radio – *4th of July*. "Maybe turn the heater down, idiot," Reed muttered to himself as he parked.

Flemington Station was busy enough, plenty of people spent time at the racecourse, and Reed slowed as he joined the foot traffic, people in coats, breath steaming in the chill air, their expressions harried as they rushed to make the platform.

While he waited for the mid-morning press to depart, Reed bought a salad roll and chewed through it until the ticket window was clear. The man had sighed and just pulled out a magazine as Reed arrived.

"Hi there," Reed said.

The fellow flipped the mag closed. "Morning."

"I'm hoping you can help me – were you working here two days ago, early evening?"

"Why?" his expression grew wary.

"Because I'm trying to find a girl, about sixteen. She was maybe busking – I need to know if she tried to buy a ticket and to where."

"Oh. The cops already asked; no idea."

"So you were working then and never saw her?"

"I was and like I said, I didn't see her."

"Anyone else working with you?"

"Sure, but they're not in now."

"Great. Could I come back and speak to them?"

The man glanced back to his screen, presumably at a schedule. "Dean is back tonight if you want to come out here again."

Damn it; that was a waste of time. "Thanks, then." Reed gave him a nod as he left. Commuters must have seen her... but who? It'd take all hours to sift through everyone and CCTV footage wasn't something he could just look over. *Besides, Duong would have mentioned if anything had been caught on film.*

There was still the golf course but he really *did* need to contact Aunty 'Mona' since he'd already put it off for too long.

"Wish I knew what she wanted," he said as he climbed back into his car.

***

Reed filled his kitchen sink then dug around his pocket for a coin – and, finding a ten cent piece, flipped it into the water with a plop. He could have called her with the hourglass in his study, or a handful of other ways, but he'd gone to the kitchen first so that was that.

"With this token I call upon Mors," he said. "Let her hear my mortal voice, a whisper across water."

The room grew colder.

Reed turned to find his aunt standing in the living room, her ever-present inky robe and silver shawl rather elegant where they fell in slender folds. Of course, the grim skull regarding him sort of ruined the effect. The depthless black eye-sockets seemed to hold no emotion at all. There was the barest hint of a face within the structure of bones, framed by regal, flowing black hair. And yet, no matter how close he came to truly seeing her, the skull always reimposed itself.

He glanced to his fishbowl... and sighed.

Gouldenstein was floating upside down; it happened nearly every time she visited – something died. Thankfully this time it was only a goldfish, but it was at least one reason he didn't have any other pets and he always kept the door locked before he called her.

"Reed."

"Aunty. How goes the harvesting of life?"

"Well enough." She glided closer. "I must apologize for sending Maximilian, but there is some urgency. Still, I did not wish to simply impose and as you know, there is always the chance of accidents."

"I understand," he said with a smile. Her politeness was somehow as amusing as it was disconcerting. "Is something wrong?"

"Yes. Something... new is occurring. Humans – Lesser Humans – I should add, are meddling with ancient magic."

She has quite the way with words sometimes. 'Lesser Humans' being those unlike Reed himself. Essentially true, he supposed, but a little uncharitable. But her news was enough to raise his pulse a little. "What magic?"

"They are compelling my children to do their bidding – well, only one, for now."

Reed frowned. *That's got to be a lot worse than it sounds.* "Do you mean a human is forcing one of your children to kill for them?"

"That is exactly what I am saying. And worse, after sending Valen to investigate this disturbance, I can no longer communicate with, much less locate, him. You must help me. As mostly human, *you* can hunt down those responsible and rescue him."

He blinked. "Can I?"

"Yes. You have gifts beyond those of a normal man, despite how you tend to ignore them."

"I suppose."

She waved her skeletal hand toward his laptop and then the drawer where he kept his handgun. "Further, you have human skills and weapons. And then there's the happy accident of your very birth."

"Happy accident?"

"Of course – I shouldn't have to remind you of the rudimentary rules."

He nodded slowly. She probably referred to the fact that neither she nor her children could remain in the world of the living for extended periods, among other unbreakable Bindings laid down by Jupiter and his Forefathers – like personally taking someone 'early'. As a human given a few 'gifts' from Death, he faced no such time limits and fewer restrictions on his dealing of life and death.

"Your existence is most convenient at times, Reed."

"I find it pretty convenient myself," Reed said. "And I'm flattered once more, to hear how my birth was a 'happy accident' but I see what you're saying now. What I'm worried about is that these humans clearly have significant power of their own if they can compel Valen. Are you sure I'm up to the task?"

Bones creaked in her approximation of a grin. "I am certain of it."

Chapter 4.

Reed abandoned his golf bag and ignored the frost-covered sign above the empty flowerbeds, slipping through them and into the trees. Here, the poplars had shed their leaves and now only black, sullen branches remained. Overhead, they scratched across the leaden sky but beneath the glistening trunks more branches lay scattered, like as-yet undiscovered victims.

And a little ways down the narrow trail, he was turning toward what was Elise's 'dump site'.

Shitful phrase, that one.

Or at least, he hoped he was walking the right way – he hadn't found anything yet. *Not that I ever have that much luck with Echoes.* But there was always a chance the tiny pulse of darkness he sensed was leading him in the right direction. And practising his special 'skills' wasn't going to kill him.

He couldn't even manage a groan or a smile at his own poor joke.

He needed more than Elise's last words or vague sightings at a train station. It still seemed that the murderer was someone rich; a drug dealer or otherwise, but that was so little to go on. *And don't forget the first rule: no assumptions.*

If he was going to continue to be honest with himself, which, sadly, sometimes he had to be – his little trip into the trees was far less daunting than what Aunty Mona expected of him. She'd given a location to check and promised the help of her children, but that location was some ways out of the city, and it would have to wait until he'd prepared properly. Just because he was not fully human didn't mean he couldn't die.

Reed turned down a muddy path – lots of footprints here.

The chill air latched onto the exposed skin of his hands and face. *I need one of auntie's shawls. Or my scarf.* And then a glimmer of yellow-tape off in the trees caught his eye; there where the dark pulse seemed stronger. "Here we go." Reed avoided the mud as best he could, crossing the damp grass and dead leaves. When he reached the site he stepped over the police tape and crouched. Not much to see; more boot marks and churned leaves.

No trace of her remained – at least, no mortal traces.

Reed knelt. Damp began to seep through his jeans but he ignored it, closing his eyes to even out his breathing. Instead, he waited, opening himself to the world. The deep silence of the realm of the Dead drew near, dark pulses intensifying. He fought the urge to tense up, to reach for and grip it, to show it away – instead, he opened his palms.

Something flickered in his mind's eye.

Black shoes, tan soles...

And then it was gone. He sighed. Not much of a clue. Chasing the Echoes that lingered around death had never been easy – and by their weakness, it was certain this was a secondary site.

A branch broke.

Reed spun.

A man leapt from the trees, knife raised. Reed fell back, catching the man's wrist as they crashed to the hard ground. The unshaven fellow growled as he straddled Reed, striving to drive the blade down.

Reed fought to keep the weapon away from his face. The stranger brought both hands to the task and his superior weight bore the point closer to Reed's eye. The man's neck muscles bulged as he fought. Reed gasped; it was a losing battle.

Do something, you idiot.

Reed kicked at the man but the creep absorbed the blows without flinching.

Something better!

He had no choice. Cripple or be killed. Reed focused on the man's snarling gaze and pushed his awareness into the pupils, like parting water, and there lay the man's future as it currently stood, stretching before him for another dozen years only. Not a long lifespan really, but his assailant didn't know that.

And yet, the poor bastard would still feel what was to come.

Reed gripped the lifespan, represented as a spreading tree with shimmering white leaves and plucked a single leaf free – taking a day from his assailant, reducing the man's lifespan by twenty-four hours. The time flowed through the man's hands and into his own. Reed couldn't stop a shiver; he'd absorbed the day. His own life was now extended beyond what was natural.

The thug flinched, his eyes widening in shock. He began to tremble, the pressure on the blade lessening... but it did not last. Reed's attacker frowned, as if brushing off a bad dream, and he pushed harder.

"I know you felt that," Reed said. "Give up or I take another day."

"What?"

Reed dragged more from the man – pulling too hard, and this time taking a small branch – equivalent to a whole week now.

The thug's whole body shuddered. He screamed, the shrill sound echoing amongst the poplars. Tears formed. Confusion and terror lay within his gaze and now the fellow attempted to draw away.

Reed squeezed harder. The flesh on his hands grew transparent, bones showing where he held the man.

"What are you?" The words came out as a shriek between short gasps.

"Unless you want me to take the rest of your lifespan, you'd better answer me," Reed said. He kept his voice cold, dispassionate, despite the revulsion twisting like a worm in his gut.

"Anything!"

"Who sent you?"

"No names." The man tripped over his words in his haste. "Never names, I'm not stupid."

"Describe him."

"Silver hair. Broken nose, shit, that's it. He wore sunglasses and a suit, you know?"

"His exact words."

"Ah, he said, something like 'follow an old blue Thunderbird and kill whoever gets out' and uh, he wanted it to be untraceable to me. I've worked for him before."

"He say why?"

"No!"

So was the hit related to Valen or Elise? Either way, Reed was going to find out. "How do you contact him?"

"Someone just turns up and takes me to him."

"Where?"

The man swallowed, then shook his head. "Please, man. Oh, Jesus, don't do it again. I can't feel *that* again."

Reed shook the hit-man until the knife fell, thudding against the cold leaves. "Tell me or I will."

"I'm dead if I do, you know that."

"That's not my problem – you chose this life. Speak," he snapped.

The thug shook his head again, writhing to escape, but Reed held on. He took another day. A second scream and the man stopped fighting; his frame fell limp as he gasped.

"Tell me and I will set you free," Reed offered.

"The Old Royal bar."

Reed released the man, who was now sobbing softly, then stood to kick the knife out of reach. He hesitated then. Sure, the guy had tried to kill him but something about seeing a person reduced to such abject fear... well, it didn't cost Reed anything to offer a shred of compassion. "Get running, pal. And I don't want to see you ever again, understood?"

"I'll be dead anyway," he said, voice tight.

"We'll see about that. I might just take care of your silver-haired friend for myself."

A flicker of hope crossed the man's face.

"Go," Reed said again, taking half a step forward.

The fellow scrambled to his feet, boots scraping dark lines in the loam, and sprinted off into the tree trunks, panting as he did. Reed watched until the man's body receded, then turned back for the green.

"Shit."

Chapter 5.

Reed waited in the Bay City golf shop while the blond woman on the desk worked on returning his deposit. It seemed to be taking a moment, which was fine, since the extra time to just continue to breathe and calm down was more than welcome. When she finally handed the money over, her expression revealed a slight distaste, mostly hidden beneath a cool, courteous exterior that matched her uniform; white polo top and short skirt of blue.

He ignored her disapproval.

"I hope you found the course suitable, despite the poor weather," she said.

"It was certainly quiet," he replied. Not unlike the shop itself, with he being the only customer.

"Of course." She paused. "Is there anything else?"

There was but she was hardly the one to help him – getting a hold of a member list wasn't going to be thanks to 'Veronica'. He needed another approach, someone he could charm, bribe or intimidate.

Or, he could blunder right in and see what happened?

"Actually, I couldn't quite stay on the course around hole eleven and when I went searching for my ball I came across what looked like police tape in the trees."

She raised a thin eyebrow. "How unfortunate. Were you able to reclaim your ball?"

"Eventually, yeah. I hope nothing sinister is afoot? I want to bring back my friends for a round but if it's dangerous?" He waited.

Finally, Veronica gave a short sigh. "Just an overdose, some kid. You don't have to worry, Mr O'Connell."

"Ah, okay, good to know," he said. "Thanks again."

Back in the carpark Reed glanced around but found only toffs and rich kids, their gleaming cars like badges, like screaming declarations.

'David O'Connell' would indeed have to come back to the Bay City golf club but not just yet – things were moving a little too fast all of a sudden, but then, that was how attempted murder always tended to make him feel.

***

Reed paced his living room as the afternoon waned.

Too bad he'd gotten rid of his boxing bag. Kicking the crap out of something would have felt good now. Real good. And it wasn't the attack as much as having his hand forced. 'Liberating' a few days here and there, as his father used to term it, wasn't so bad if the ends were just. *Doesn't mean I have to like it precisely either.*

And he'd probably use the days for something worthwhile eventually... if he could get ahead somehow. But for now, those extra leaves would have to be added to the others he'd taken over the years. The total wasn't in any danger of getting out of hand but it wasn't something he could make a habit of – another old rule. *After all, the more I do that the more I leave loved ones behind.* He glanced around the empty, quiet apartment. *Not exactly a big problem for you right now, is it?*

And there were other rules – rules the gods had handed down about Reapers and taking people early; that one bore heavy consequences. He slumped into his armchair with a sigh.

Somewhere along the way in his short investigation, he'd come too close to something. A piece of knowledge, a name or a place, *something* had certainly made someone uncomfortable.

Either that or he was way off and the attack was actually linked to Valen.

And wasn't that quite the pickle?

The fair trip out of the city and to Hanfield didn't appeal right now – but if he wanted answers, that night club the thug mentioned might just be the place to start. Either that or push the issue with the police. And maybe the Old Royal wasn't the right way just yet – maybe Duong was a better bet. *He won't be able to reopen the case but maybe there's something on the tape from the train station.*

Elise deserved a proper investigation.

But not before tomorrow – his limbs were like lead pipes attached to a frozen ham, even without the shock of 'liberating days', winter was a real prick. He hauled himself into the hallway to hit the button for the central heating then paused at the sound of soporific television banter. Reed tensed – he hadn't left the television on.

A sharp voice echoed in disagreement with a commercial

and Reed sighed. Maximilian.

Reed strode into the kitchen to get a drink, where he collected his orange juice and moved into the living room. Max sat in an armchair, one ankle crossed over his knee. He still wore his leathers with the plain white T beneath, *Grease*-style hair and big sunglasses. Today, however, he wore a green scarf.

"Geez, you look a bit seedy, don't you?" Max observed.

"Do I?" Reed took the couch. "So you're here to help. What have you got?"

"Straight to business then? You're in a bad mood."

"You got that right." He explained the case, his failure to get very far and the attack at the golf course. "I had to take some of his Time; I don't like it."

"Ah yes, your famous reluctance to embrace your heritage."

"Can we move along, already?"

"Of course. Hanfield is a small place with an ageing population so we've all been there a fair few times over the last decade. Everything about it was routine but when Valen went to check on the strange 'waves' mother noticed, he sent a message back and then disappeared. We haven't heard from him since – it's been a week now and mother forbade us from following at first."

"And the message?"

"That humans were abusing the natural order of things, that they sought to wake something that has slept for hundreds of years."

Reed leant forward. "I don't like the sound of that."

"Nor I. From that rather vague missive, it could be any number of things. Bad things, Reed."

"Just what the world needs, more scum."

"Well, Mother sent me to help so you've got me as long as I'm able to stay on your side. Then it's back to work so let's not waste time."

Which meant anywhere from minutes to days, really. But Max would be a big help, if he could stay on the right track. "All right. So, we have to go to Hanfield, right?"

"And you want to just walk in there? Welcome to the Wild West."

"Let's stop in some of the surrounding spots and ask a few questions then decide what to do. You can tell me if anyone lies to us and if you feel any more of those 'waves' you mentioned."

"Is this how you do your private eye-ing?"

Now he grinned. "Not always – sometimes I make it up as I go."

Chapter 6.

On the freeway more black tree trunks flashed by, sharp like forgotten rifles standing beneath an overcast sky.

Reed kept an eye on a white van that seemed to follow from a few car lengths back. Barely an hour out of the city and they were probably being trailed. Perfect. Was it someone come to finish what the thug had failed to do at the golf course? The van was not a very remarkable vehicle. But it kept its distance, took all the same exits and didn't try to pass, even when Reed slowed, just enough to be a minor inconvenience to the surrounding drivers.

"Notice that white van back there?" he asked Max.

Max looked up from the copy of Playboy he was reading. "I thought they got rid of the nudity – it's back."

"Where did you even get that?" Reed asked. "And did you hear what I said – I think someone is following us."

His cousin shrugged. "I might be dead in some sense of the word, but it doesn't mean I don't get lonely. And how do you think you were conceived? It wasn't a stork, you know."

Reed groaned. "It's like I'm talking to a shoe."

Max glanced to the passenger mirror. "I see them. So what?"

"So it could be a lead – watch them, can you?"

"Fine." He tossed the magazine onto the back seat. "What about this first stop then, whatever it's called, what are we asking exactly?"

"If anyone has seen an angelic-looking young man pass through."

"I wouldn't go that far. I mean, he's blond and pretty, awfully white too, I suppose but he's no angel. Once, we were sneaking into Mars' bedchamber –"

"Max."

"Fine. What if no-one saw him?"

"Then we visit the local police and ask about any disturbances."

He put his feet up on the dashboard – at some point, he'd removed his shoes. And socks. "And these waves mother was talking about? I know she's hoping your human part will be immune or some such, but what about me?"

"Pass the Fringe if it gets too dangerous."

"Yeah." The word sounded quite flat.

He glanced at his cousin. "You're worried, aren't you?"

"Very much."

Reed grimaced, gripping the wheel as he turned into the exit that would get them to Hanfield and the smaller towns nearby. Not many things bothered the children of Death. "I kind of wish you'd lied."

***

Hanfield was typically quiet, one petrol station and a motel on the edge of town, a single row of shops and then houses and gardens. It was actually quite neat, rows of hunkered marigolds around a central lawn where a few people were eating their lunch beneath the paltry winter sun.

Reed pulled up across from an ATM and glanced around.

Half a dozen people moving between shops, a cafe and a sporting store, what had to be one of the last DVD rental places in the state, and a *Just Jeans*. And not a single person bearing the harried look of people dealing with serious underworld upheaval. "Can you feel anything?" Reed asked.

Max shook his head. "No, damn it."

"What?"

"This was a waste of time," he said, waving a hand at the main street. "There's nothing here – just like the other towns, they've already moved on, I can feel the Echoes."

A touch of relief settled – no giant showdown with unknown dread forces then. "And Valen?"

"He's one of them."

"Meaning?"

"They've taken him with them," Max said. He glanced to the sky. "We need to head out of town – there's a water tower."

Reed pulled from the kerb and started driving, following Max's directions, his cousin speaking in a clipped tone that did much to rebuild the tension that had briefly dissolved but moments ago.

Yet it didn't take long for the yellowed stone structure

to rise up above the trimmed lawns and clean rooves. The water tower and its iron ladder stood in a small reserve of shrubs and silver birch – and yet there were two towers, two sets of trees. He blinked when one image superimposed over the other. One set of trees were green, vibrant, one tower was tall and sturdy.

The other was a crumbling ruin, no taller than his waist.

Trees were shrivelled and black; the earth seared too, the scent of ash reaching him from where he sat in the car, staring through the open window.

The Fringe.

Land of decay that lurked between the world of Living and Death.

"Gods, what happened here?"

A click from the car door followed and Max was already walking around the car, heading for the ruin. "Help me," he called.

Reed leapt out of the Thunderbird and followed – half his footfalls hit grass, the other ash. A heavy feel to the atmosphere pressed down upon his chest, seemed to clench at his limbs, air hot when he drew it in. "Why is the Fringe so strong here?" he asked. For his human side, the Fringe was dangerous enough on its own. What else lurked near the tower?

"No idea."

Max had bent within the centre of the water tower. He sifted through the char, hands frantic. Ash sprang up around him and he coughed but didn't stop until he'd lifted something free, grey flecks falling away from a long shape.

A bundle of wood – pale birch, untouched by the flames. Each piece had been cut evenly, bound by red leather ribbon, which had also escaped burning somehow. "A Fasces?" Reed asked.

"Yes," Max said, brow furrowed. "*Strength through unity.*"

"Don't they usually have an axe head too?"

"Not always." He turned it over, then began to mutter in Latin, not loud enough for Reed to catch any of it. Then Max stood. "This is worse than we thought. Mother needs to see this."

Reed caught his cousin by the shoulders. "What does it mean?"

"See the carving here?"

Entwined vines. "I do."

"It suggests more than just unity and strength. It's for binding and I have no idea *what*, but I think I know why they have Valen at least."

"Why? And who's 'they' for that matter?"

"A Coven."

"Witches?"

"More like a Fraternity. Of fools."

Trouble, trouble, trouble. "What about your brother?"

"Whatever these bastards have summoned they're using Valen as a conduit; it's the only thing that makes sense."

Reed didn't question it – even though the conclusion went against his golden rule about assumptions – because Max knew more about summoning than most.

"Get out of town, Reed. It might not be far away."

"Where are you–?"

Max was gone.

Chapter 7.

"Play that part again, can you?" Reed asked. "Right before she leaves."

Reed leaned closer to the laptop, wrinkling his nose at Duong's cigarette. It was definitely Veronica from the Bay City Golf Course, same sneer, same hair; and she passed Elise without stopping. But after a few moments the girl set her acoustic guitar down, closed the lid of her case and strolled in the direction Veronica had left. *Maybe finding that guitar would help too.*

"What about it?" Duong asked.

"That woman works at the golf course and Elise followed her."

He narrowed his eyes. "You sure? It's not exactly crystal clear HD... could you be mistaken about the woman?"

"I'm sure."

"Shit." He slapped the desk. "If you're right, I should have seen this."

"Was it a priority round here?" Reed asked pointedly.

Duong jammed his cigarette in the ashtray, then lifted

the plastic desk plant up and hid the tray. "I said *if* you're right."

Reed glanced at the plant. "Can't people smell it?"

He shrugged. "If they do, no-one has complained yet and it's been four years."

Reed turned back to the screen, to the empty place where Elise had stood. "You've been to the course, you didn't interview Veronica?"

"I've got her statement but one of the constables probably spoke to her. Not much to follow up on... or so we thought," he said with a troubled frown.

"Well I'm glad I've brought you a lead. You're heading that way, right?"

"Right." He scooped up the keys to his cruiser.

"Then you won't mind if I escort you to there."

"*You're* escorting *me*?"

"Yep."

"Look, you've probably saved us some face here but this is an active investigation now so if you want to stick around, rein it in."

"So, we're sharing a case again."

Duong grunted. "Better than having you slink around after me, I guess."

"Slink?"

"Slink."

"Well." Reed folded his arms even as he grinned. "I was going to let you pretend you broke the case and everything but now I'm having second thoughts."

"Come on."

The drive from the inner-city station to Bay City took longer than it needed to of course, but that was traffic –

crammed between the buildings, a maze of glass windows dark in the shade, exhaust and talk radio; good times. He tapped his foot on the passenger floor as they crawled along, and when the orange blink of a sign joyously proclaiming Roadworks Ahead appeared, he groaned. It wasn't just the traffic – he still hadn't heard from Max, or anyone in the family. Just what had been summoned? Was Valen still 'alive' or had something worse happened? There were limits to what Aunty could do, eons-old rules... but would she step in more 'personally' if things got out of hand?

Hasn't happened ever *before.*

He sighed. *Focus!* Elise deserved his full attention now.

"You right over there?" Duong asked, eyes still on the road.

"Just impatient," he said. "I think this is the one; she's involved, I can feel it."

"What about your rule?"

"Hmmm. Want to run the siren?"

"You know that won't work."

"True. What about this – wake me when we get there."

Duong laughed. "It's ten more minutes."

"Perfect."

***

A smarmy smile attached to a tanned man greeted them at the reception, his blue shirt complimenting the artificial violets arranged on the bench. "I'm afraid Veronica isn't in today, Detective."

"I see. And do you expect her back today?"

"She sounded quite ill on the phone."

Duong made a note in his notebook. "When was this?"

"I'm not sure – sometime this morning."

"Thank you." Duong started for the carpark, stepping around the small queue that had formed behind them. He glanced to Reed as the automatic doors slid open. "What do you think about that?"

Reed shivered at the blast of cold air. "Could be a coincidence... but I think I should head back inside soon, just in case she's hidden herself in the back room, don't you?"

"Very much so."

"What about you?"

"Going to run a check on Miss Hannington. Meet you in the car."

Reed set off with a nod, heading up along the reception wall, passing beneath high windows. A series of rose bushes shielded him from any potentially curious golfers heading down to Hole One as he approached a second pair of sliding glass doors.

He slowed, crouching to listen.

A small group of golfers were exiting, engrossed in their discussion about falling stock prices. "Come on, Veronica, you're in there, I know it," he muttered beneath his breath.

But no voices followed from within.

Smarmy didn't call out, laugh nor pick up the phone, it was simply quiet. Reed closed his eyes a moment – were they whispering? He gave it a little more time before creeping further forward and parting the rose bushes enough to see through the glass.

Smarmy, the smarmy bastard, was the only one inside.

Were they simply being prudent, waiting until Duong's

cruiser left the course?

Or was Veronica truly ill?

"Reed?"

He flinched, scratching his forearm on a thorn as he turned. Duong stood behind him, an eyebrow raised. "You drop some small change?"

"No, but if you find any let me know." Reed stood. "I don't think she's here. "Anything turn up at your end?"

"Nothing interesting. We better go visit her at home, I think."

"Somewhere close by, right?"

"Hawthorn."

Only twenty minutes... traffic depending, of course. "Fine."

***

Veronica Hannington's terrace house was a narrow, two-storey building with a four-foot-deep front 'yard' ringed by concrete. A flower box rested in the upper storey window. It did not contain flowers but instead, what appeared to be action figures. A weathered Buzz Lightyear and a couple of Teenage Mutant Ninja Turtles. *Didn't know the Turtles were back in fashion.*

The detective rested a hand on the gate. "Don't rush this in there."

"Do I look like an imbecile?" Reed snapped.

Duong raised an eyebrow. "That's quite a nasty mood you've got going."

"Sorry, lots on my mind."

"Anything you need to share before we go in there and potentially risk our lives?"

"Our lives?"

The policeman folded his arms as he stared at the home. "You never know what's going to be behind the door. I learnt that the hard way, long time ago."

"Well, when you put it that way."

"So, is there something I need to know about?"

"Nope."

"Fine. Me first." Duong started up the steps and knocked on the door. "Miss Hannington?"

No answer.

Reed stretched out and pressed the doorbell. A jangling followed but still no-one answered.

"I'll try the front window then," he said.

"You're not breaking in, Reed."

"You'd make a terrible down-on-his-luck private investigator, you know?"

Duong didn't answer, instead pulling his phone and dialling.

Reed stepped around the front step and into the garden bed, peering between open curtains. A study lay inside, a cluttered desk with laptop resting there, lid closed. But a hallway was visible through an open door and it revealed a motionless figure. Blonde hair. He leaned closer – it could easily be Veronica.

"Duong, kick the door open or something," he called.

"What?"

"There's someone lying in the hall – if they were okay, they'd have gotten up by now."

"That the truth?"

"Come and see if you want," Reed said as he turned from the window.

Instead, the sound of something striking wood followed. He reached the door just as it flung inward with a crack of splintered wood, where it hung from one hinge. Duong pulled his gun and stalked into the house. He knelt before the figure then called over his shoulder. "Check her."

Then he was moving deeper into the townhouse, weapon still held before him.

Reed crouched over the woman... Veronica. Her eyes were empty and a thin trail of blood ran from one nostril. She still wore her Bay City uniform and the scent of a floral perfume lingered.

No hint about the manner of her death either, no marks on her throat, blood in her hair or on her clothes, none seeping from beneath her torso.

Doung's footsteps started up toward the loft and Reed leant closer, placing his hands over one of Veronica's – and closed his eyes to let the drab, muteness that filled her body guide him through her fingertips and along her limb to pass through the now stone-like heart and to her throat and mouth, where the tongue lay flat and still.

"In the name of Mors, speak any that you might," he whispered. "I will help you."

Unlike Elise, Veronica's body seemed only too willing to answer – not unusual for someone who had only recently died, but the words were soft.

He moved closer still.

"Maybe it was something I ate. I'm sure I'll be in tomorrow."

And then the rasping voice was gone.

He straightened. Not much to go on, but the obvious possibility was poison, surely? Of course, his old rule echoed in his mind – assume nothing.

Duong called down from upstairs. "The place is empty. I'm calling the ambulance."

"Right."

Reed ducked into an adjoining room, an empty kid's room. There, a blanket rested upon the foot of the bed; he returned to drape it over her body.

One thing was growing clear now: Elise's murder was bigger than it first seemed.

Chapter 8.

Reed leant against the cold of the low stone fence, waiting for Doung to finish with the ambulance. Its flashing lights were odd in daylight, barely colouring the surrounding buildings or the gathered crowd across the narrow street. For some reason, people were filming the scene on their mobiles.

A remarkably short figure dressed in an army-green coat and hoodie appeared from between the onlookers, shadowed face seeming to stare across at Reed. Reed straightened when he saw what appeared to be black, fingerless mittens on the figure's hands.

"Reed, I'm following the ambulance," Duong said as he approached.

"All right, keep me posted then."

"Not coming along? We'll know if your poison theory pans out if I can rush the autopsy."

"No, I want to watch the crowd a little longer, see if anyone interesting turns up."

"I think it's a waste of time."

He smiled. "But you believe you can rush the autopsy?"

"Humph. Good luck then," the detective said, motioning to one of the crime scene technicians as he moved toward his car. Reed started across the street, pausing for a taxi, heading for the short stranger.

Based on the mittens there was a good chance the fellow wasn't a man at all but a Grub, one of Pluto's vaguely humanoid servants. Even as the grub turned away, pushing through the bystanders in search of quieter surrounds, Reed couldn't help a rueful smile. *Grub.* Quite an uncharitable name. *Especially considering what they harvest.*

The grub found an alley half-buried in a riot of graffiti and the hulking form of a large blue bin, black plastic bags of rubbish peeking from above the rim. The creature turned and pulled back the hood, revealing a flat face with wide set eyes – a little too wide to be mistaken for human perhaps, not to mention the complete lack of iris or the earthy tint to the skin.

"Something big is happening underground; I've been told to bring you there."

"By who?" Reed asked.

A slight frown crossed the wide lips. "One of your family... Mr Leather and Sunglasses, it was."

So Max is safe – that's something, at least. "Right. What's wrong?"

"Best if I show you," the grub said, turning toward the rear of the alley.

Reed caught its shoulder, cold, cold flesh beneath the army jacket. "Hold on. Does it have to do with the murders I'm investigating or whatever's going on with Valen?"

"You tell us." He kept moving, soon stopping at the end of the alley. "You ready? I know this isn't pleasant for you, since you're the Half-Skull."

Touché, little Grub. "I'll just need a moment on the other side."

"Understood."

The grub knelt and plunged both mittens – or perhaps 'appendages' was a better description – into the ground. They passed through the stone and steam rose... but drew forth no scent, no real damage.

Reed glanced over his shoulder but no-one was near.

Had a 'normal' approached, they wouldn't have noticed the grub piercing the Fringe but they might have taken a few steps back if they saw Reed simply disappear. *Not that those poor souls tended to be believed whenever it's reported in any event.*

Once the grey, shimmering portal was wide enough, the grub rose and stepped within. Reed approached, tensing up with each step – he didn't have time to take any of the usual precautions, even with the grub as guide – but still took a breath and jumped after. A silent wind buffeted him yet he floundered in place, even as he was tossed around as if by giant hands or the breath of Gods. It was always that way and his stomach lurched.

He didn't open his eyes.

Best not to risk it – the things he saw tended to linger.

And then the wind died away and a welcome stillness fell across him, drawing him close and he was standing. Unlike at the water tower, when the Fringe had simply bled forth in what would be a temporary intrusion on the world of the living, here, it was a matter of using the Fringe in order to skip through earth and stone, and *that* was a little more disconcerting.

He swallowed, breathing deep while his stomach settled and finally opened his eyes not to the Fringe, but to a large cavern... no, the darkened walls were *concrete* and up ahead, a bolt of light slid down from above, illuminating more graffiti; pinks and yellows proclaiming nothing, as far as Reed could tell.

Aside from gangs and cave dwellers, urban explorers and homeless folk who spent a lot of time beneath Melbourne's streets, there were sometimes darker, hungrier things, things usually happy to stay hidden. *Aside from the occasional visit topside to fuel conspiracy theories or snatch bodies after building collapses, I suppose.* Was that what he was going to have to face?

"Where are we now?" Reed asked as the grub knelt beside him, rubbing at the damp concrete in order to close the tear in the Fringe.

"Below St Paul's Cathedral."

"So, are we going to bump into Jesus?"

The Grub snorted. "Very funny. Besides, the Master says *he's* stuck somewhere in Rome at the moment; he's a busy fellow, you know. Lots of his priests to chastise."

"Good to hear."

"So, we need to go a little deeper, follow me."

The grub started down the echoing drain, stubby legs walking swiftly enough, though Reed didn't have to tax himself in order to keep up. They soon came to a steel ladder heading down.

"Not far now," Pluto's servant said as he started climbing.

Reed followed, a chill sneaking up from below. Each rung seemed colder than the last but at least they weren't caked in rust. Maintenance crews probably used it – but he didn't find anything of the sort below.

He fell back against the ladder.

A writhing mass of black and red pulsed where it seemed to have driven itself into the stone walls, as if trying to – worm-like – tunnel free of the drain. Was it seeking the Cathedral or hoping to escape it? The thing filled the drain, almost a storey tall but there was no discernible head, face or even body truly – it was simply a pent-up concentration of bitterness, terror, jealousy and half a dozen other negative emotions... the sense of them washed over him like mighty scents: grapefruit, chilli and honey.

It didn't make sense of course, but his parents had told him, long ago that his human side sometimes struggled to process certain things from beyond the Fringe. *Watch out for Rage, that one can make your bloody eyes water*, Dad had said.

The vast thing wasn't alone – scores of grubs swarmed over its surface, their lighter bodies tainted red or black by the glow, as their cloven hands dug at the mass, wide mouths gnashing. *Almost like maggots, really – only for spirits*.

And it wasn't too far off the truth; Pluto's minions served an important purpose when it came to spiritual debris... yet the size of the worm was unprecedented, even for a city.

"Can you actually handle this thing?" Reed asked.

The grub chuckled. "Of course. More of my brethren are on their way. We'll deal with this lump – the problem you've been asked to deal with is *why* it formed in the first place. It is, after all, a human problem when you think about it."

Reed shook his head. "I think this is a little above my salary."

"The Masters don't seem to think so," the Grub said. "Besides, you know how lazy they are. They'd just as soon have you or someone similar deal with it."

"Wonderful."

"Well, I've shown you now – so I'd better get back to work, good luck, Mr Lavender."

The Grub scurried off, throwing itself somewhat gleefully into the body of the spirit-worm, emitting little whoops of joy. Reed sighed. As disgusting as it was, the grubs were part of a process that Normals simply never saw or appreciated – though obviously quite similar to the decay of physical bodies.

Any negative emotion the grubs devoured was stored in their stomach to slowly turn a bright blue as it changed – and even as Reed continued to shake his head at the mess he'd been given to deal with, a line of grubs with glowing stomachs of azure formed, heading for the surface.

There, they'd sneak into the city and release Hope, Joy, Determination and all the other things humanity needed to meet the challenge of each new day. When he'd seen the grubs in the past, they were usually skipping back from hospitals.

"Got any of that good stuff for me, boys?"

Chapter 9.

Reed paced, glass of milk in hand, cold kitchen tiles beneath his socks – no-one was responding to his calls, not Duong and not anyone from 'the family' either. And it had been hours now. He paused at the whine of a siren; drawing near swiftly, clear over the hum of traffic. Yet even if he glanced out the kitchen window to the darkening courtyard below it wouldn't help; whoever had been sent to deal with the any deceased would be too busy to talk.

"Come on, *someone* must be free."

He needed answers.

More than a few balls were up in the air now; Elise, Veronica, the Fasces and the Coven and now the spirit-worm and its bitter darkness... and everywhere dead-ends to go with the dead bodies. He grimaced as he ran a glass of water. *Poor pun there, Reed.* Duong would likely be waiting for the autopsy, working on Veronica's financial details, her phone records, interviewing family... actual hard work.

But I'm looking for a shortcut, aren't I? It was true – he needed a new lead, an actual suspect, anything, really, and right away. It was time to try something a little irregular. At least, irregular for most people.

Because all he had were a handful of facts, half-truths and guesses.

Elise had left home with very little. She'd been murdered then taken to the golf course, possibly after meeting and following Veronica, an employee of said course. A week or two later, Veronica had rebuffed him and was possibly poisoned... for being seen speaking to the police? Or something else?

And Valen's disappearance and the threat posed by the mysterious coven, the silence from Max and Aunty, did any of that have anything to do with the spirit-worm? The grubs didn't know, and why would they? Pluto wasn't going to give them such information, *if* he even knew – or, more likely, if he even *cared*.

"Time to take a little risk."

Reed set his glass down and strode to the bedroom, glancing at the hastily made bed as he opened the wardrobe and shifted a few boxes – mostly books –then drew forth a long, thin chest.

His mother's handwriting, in the *mortscript*, spanned the lid – proclaiming it the resting place for the Coda. He ran his fingertips across the words a moment, then pulled his keychain free, taking a tiny key and unlocking the chest.

The lid creaked as it opened, revealing blue velvet lining that cradled a bone horn yellowed with age, the mouthpiece a bright silver. "Ready to sing again?" he asked the Coda as he stepped into the en-suite, jammed the plug into the bath and ran the hot tap. Then he swung the door shut with his foot and leant against the basin bench, folding his arms to wait for steam.

It took a while but once the mirror behind him had fogged over, Reed took a breath and raised the horn to his lips... and paused. Calling the dead was a little different to evoking final words – for one, it was essentially quite rude.

And there were a few measures worth taking, such as the room and the steam. *Give a ghost a room and she'll take the house,* was something his mother had always said. Reed's gaze fell upon the hot tap. Steam – only while it lingered would his visitor actually stay this side of the Fringe... but that didn't mean the spirit wouldn't try something untoward. They often did, especially when Reed called them.

It's all that warm, comfortable flesh, right?

I need answers.

He sounded the note.

A quavering peal rang out across the Fringe – it was a dim, thin sound but in the bathroom, in his apartment, there was only the rush of his breath. He lowered the Coda.

Once was enough.

A shape began to form in the steam, hovering above the tap – a child perhaps? Washed of colour, it seemed to be a blonde girl with bobbed hair, longer at the front, her expression joyous. She wore a floral print dress but as she stretched a hand forth in wonder, he caught a glimpse of an Avril Lavigne bracelet.

"Where am I?" she asked, her voice echoing. She glanced around with wide eyes and her disbelief caused a twang of guilt.

The adults were always better; they understood immediately.

"In my bathroom," he said. "I've called you because I need

your help; my name is Reed and Mors is my aunty. Do you remember her?"

The girl nodded.

"What's your name?"

"Lily." Now she frowned and her eyes lost focus a moment. "I don't understand. I thought I was... the car..."

"You still are," he said, softly.

Her shoulders slumped. "Oh."

"Lily, do you understand the rules?"

She opened her mouth to reply but did not speak; instead she craned her neck up, as though listening to someone above her. Reed checked on the water lever; he didn't have endless amount of time, unless he wanted to flood his apartment.

Lily looked back to him. "I think I do. You have to do something I ask."

"Right. Once you help me, I help you."

"Can you bring me back?"

"I'm not allowed," he replied. "But I can give someone a message or even do something for you, if you like?"

She sighed. "You first, Mister Lavender."

"All right. I'm trying to solve a crime – a young woman named Elise Roberts was murdered. Can you see anything that would help me?"

"Do you want me to ask Elise?"

"That's not allowed."

"What do you mean? I can try and find her. I'm sure it won't take me long, Mister Lavender."

He glanced back at the water – the bath was only half full. Still, explaining the rules around balance, power and the not unreasonable limits set upon the amount of control the living were permitted to exert over the dead, simply wasn't on the cards. "Thanks Lily, but Aunty doesn't permit that. One summoning only – just you and I can talk."

"So, you mean you can't... call anyone you want to talk to, it's like, random?"

"Very. But all you have to do is sort of listen and concentrate and see if you notice anything." He held back a sigh; it wasn't Lily's fault she hadn't had any practice, in fact, *he* was imposing upon her.

"I'll do my best." She closed her eyes and her face wavered in the steam.

Reed tapped a finger against his thigh but managed to avoid pacing the small room. When Lily opened her eyes it was to hop in place.

"I found something!"

"Fantastic," Reed said with a smile.

"It was hard to hear, like a crackly radio but it was something about the movies and there was a name too... Girabaldi."

"Girabaldi, that's great," Reed said. "About the movies, do you mean like at an actual cinema?"

"Yeah... I think it was the Cinema Nova. Does that help?"

"Absolutely," Reed said. It might not have been much, but it was better than nothing. "Now, what can I do for you?"

"Well... I wasn't sure at first but can you find my brother and give him a message?"

"I'll do my best." Of course, refusal wasn't an option – any of the living who refused to hold up their end of the bargain tended to be visited by Aunty a little earlier than expected, but failure could be negotiated, at least. "What's the message, Lily? And you'd better tell me your last name, too."

"It's Stephens... but I want to save the message. Just find him first; I'll wait right here."

"Ah, that's not quite how it works, either," Reed said.

"I suppose..." Lily shrugged. "His name is Matt."

"Great. And the message?"

Lily spun, then turned back to Reed. "Someone is coming."

"Who?"

But she blinked out of sight.

Was she safe? Who had approached that would cause her to flee? More trouble, no doubt – hopefully she was safe. "I'll find a way to call you again, Lily," he said as he leant forward to cut the tap. He opened the window next, thumping the warped sill, and steam started to escape into the late afternoon air.

Reed sighed. *That was a lot easier than last time.* In some ways, at least. Whether finding Matt Stephens would be easy, let alone locating Lily once more, both tasks would have to wait for now. Cinema Nova took priority.

Or Garibaldi, perhaps.

He pulled the plug and returned to the kitchen while the porcelain began its distorted guzzling. There, he ran a glass of water and drank, the chill welcome after the mini steam room. He wiped at the sweat that had formed at his temples, then removed his jacket.

"You're not supposed to do that, you know."

Reed jumped, spinning to find Max leaning against the opposite wall – this time, his sunglasses were hooked over the neck of his shirt, revealing golden, almost wolf-like eyes.

"What, my job?"

"You know what I mean – Mother doesn't like it when you use the Coda. You're like us, for the most part. Can't you just put in a request for once? Or better yet, just pass the Fringe yourself."

"Yes, because that's not at all incredibly dangerous."

Max snorted. "Even if you died there, you'd only be *changed*, it's not like you'd disappear forever."

"No, I'd only be changed forever. I need my body, Cousin," Reed said with a shake of his head. "And as for your idea of a request, how long do you think that takes?"

"Well, so what? You're rushing again, like you always do, and now you owe that girl – who's fine by the way, I must have spooked her."

"That's a relief at least."

"Well, if you're so enamoured of your fleshy side that you're avoiding the Fringe so studiously, then why not let your detective friend do his job or hit the streets again yourself?"

Reed clenched his jaw. "I made a promise."

"Yeah, yeah." Max flickered out of sight. A moment of silence passed before his voice rang from the lounge room. "Want me to tell you what we found out about the Coven or not?"

Chapter 10.

Reed moved into the lounge, where Max had sprawled across the entire couch. He was flipping through an issue of *Rolling Stone*. "You still buy these paper dinosaurs even though it's all online now, right?"

Reed took the armchair, settling into its creaking, wooden bones with a grunt. "Has been for years."

"Don't you care about the environment?"

"I guess I'm clinging to a shrinking medium just to be different. Happy?"

"Maybe if you'd had a better answer."

Reed sighed. "The Coven, Max."

Max tossed the magazine onto the overburdened coffee table, where it met a dozen other issues, three empty glasses and a phone charger. "They call themselves the Shining Leaves – ridiculous name, right? – and we think they're actually trying to siphon power from Feronia, using Valen as some sort of lightning rod."

Reed straightened in his chair. "But isn't Feronia the Goddess of the wilderness and fertility and... something else? How does that work?"

"*Abundance* is the something else," Max said. "Shameful, by the way – this is your heritage."

"Very funny. And you still haven't answered how or why?"

"Well, as to the 'why' we're still not sure of it but Lina and I think we know how they're using Valen, at least."

Lina? *Hmmm...* That would mean extra work; she was altogether too friendly. "You couldn't find another cousin?"

"I'm just following Mother's orders," Max said with a grin.

"Fine – so what do you know?"

"Since we harness energy when people die and redirect it between here and the Underworld, we effectively act as conduits, right?"

"Right." The same energy was used for sending souls back into the Lifepool; all of Death's children needed to be able to manipulate such energy but if someone was interrupting that process somehow, were their folks trapped in limbo?

"So we've? come to the fairly solid assumption that these humans must lack equivalent artefacts, otherwise they'd do it themselves."

"All right, but they don't completely lack power. They didn't capture Valen with some string and a washing basket."

"That's where we three come in. We have to find out how, free Valen and then stop whatever the Coven is up to before the full moon. They're building up to something."

Reed shook his head. "Madness."

"You don't have to give up so easily, you know."

"I haven't but come on, this sounds like something for Mors to deal with, rules or no. What's to stop these Shining Leaf saps from capturing you and Lina and killing me?"

"I already asked for her to step in – she said no, like every other time." Max sat up and snapped his fingers. A skull in a bonnet appeared in place of his own face. "Surrogates only, Maximilian. That is the only way balance is maintained. We have gone over this many times."

"Nice impression. What now?" Reed said.

Max's grinning face returned. "You get some proper rest. In the morning, Lina will meet us and then we're heading further east, to a place called Emerald. It has a lake, I'm sure you've heard of it."

"I have." Reed leant forward. "You don't seem as concerned as before."

He shrugged. "Maybe because I'm pretty sure Valen is still Dead. For a while, I thought he might have been absorbed or even Vanished... but I think we have a chance now, especially if Lina finds what I think she'll find."

"Being?"

"I'll let her explain," Max said, then he sat up with a jerk. "Actually, I need to duck out for a little while."

"Work?"

His expression had lost all traces of its usual humour. "It's a bus."

"Oh."

Max disappeared halfway through the syllable so Reed stood and headed for the bedroom. Rest wasn't a bad idea at all. He'd been pushing himself hard on every damn front – and maybe Max was right about rushing too. A clear head couldn't hurt and maybe by then, Duong would have come up with something.

He kicked off his shoes and slumped onto the bed.

***

Lilac.

Reed frowned, only half aware of his own confusion as sleep lingered. Lilac – didn't that mean... He opened his eyes and blinked against light from the window, a dim shape before him.

He blinked as a pale face resolved before him, a small smile on vivid blue lips.

"You know, your nose twitches when you sleep."

He groaned. "That's not creepy at all, Lina."

She chuckled, rolling onto her back from where she'd presumably been lying beside him, watching him sleep. Her silvery hair fanned across the pillow and the sleeveless black tunic she wore rode up, revealing her thighs – awfully smooth and perhaps tinted with just the suggestion of purple.

She only wears it to make you uncomfortable and you shouldn't look anyway.

He sat up, swinging his legs around then reaching for the glass of water beside the bed, taking a long drink before rubbing at one of his shoulders – the reward of the side-sleeper.

"Max said you found something?"

"Right," she said. "There's an antiques dealer we need to visit before we go to Emerald. Smith Street Bazaar; they've been selling things to the Coven, I want to know exactly what."

"Sounds like a good starting p–"

Reed pitched forward as something hit him.

Lina's arms fell across his shoulders as she burrowed

her face into his neck, the coolness both refreshing and chilling, disturbing. "Max can catch up with us; he's still busy working on that busload of tourists, they haven't all passed yet, poor souls."

"Ah, Lina."

"You'll carry me to the Bazarr, right?"

"No, that would be... strange, in the least."

"What do you mean?"

He sighed. "You know how we've talked – many times – about humans and how we have some quite specific ideas about family and closeness?"

"We're barely cousins, Reed."

He caught her hands and gently lifted them away as he stood. "But we are."

She shrugged. "Really, it's a tenuous link. And I'm several thousand years older than you in any event, shouldn't *that* worry you more?"

"I worry about everything when you're around, Lina."

She smiled. "You're sweet to say so!"

"Give me a moment to change," he said, as he reached for the en-suite door.

"It'll be quicker if I help."

"No thanks." Reed closed the door behind him and went to the basin, bending down to splash water onto his face before straightening.

Lina grinned at him from the mirror.

He hung his head. "Are you really that bored?"

"Fine. You're beginning to become a bit of a grumpy old man, you know. Are you going to start yelling at clouds, next?"

"Just meet me in my car, will you?"

Lina disappeared.

Once he'd changed and gathered the usual items required for a trip to an antique bazaar: phone, wallet, gun and tiny silver bell with a blazing sun for a handle, it was time to head into the city. Thankfully, rush hour had come and gone.

Taking a tram might have been easier but dealing with Lina in public was difficult enough without exposing a whole heap of commuters to his cousin – as one of death's children she tended to have a dampening effect on the health of regular people. Which wasn't to say they'd die – not unless she wanted them to – but pre-existing ailments tended to flare up. Once, Valen had made some poor truckie cough up blood, just by appearing in the same queue.

Whoever cleaned the Post Office floor that day had a pretty rough time of it.

Lina was waiting in the passenger seat when he reached his car, and he hopped in and glanced at her. She gave him a nod, her expression more sombre than he'd expected, so he fired the engine and got them out of the underground parking as quick as he could.

"Something happen?" he asked as he kept an eye on the mess of cars before him. Glossy shop windows flashed as he headed toward Fitzroy.

"It's just the city. There's someone passing the Fringe all the time... Mother's had me in the countryside for a little while now. It's different there when it's mostly animals and a few humans at a time." She glanced out the window, craning her neck to look up at a skyscraper. "Here it's everything. Animals, insects, birds, humans, everything. Like that skyscraper there – one of your banks, right?"

"Right."

"There's a man hanging from his tie on the twenty-seventh floor – he's been addicted to cocaine for a decade; it's been destroying his family so he's giving them the insurance. Potter's attending."

Reed couldn't fight a tiny shiver; he'd never been able to sense death quite so clearly and the sheer relentless weight of it, the constant sadness, would probably drown him if he could... and mention of Potter wasn't exactly pleasant, either. Of all the family, Potter seemed to have the most trouble with Reed's very existence. "It still gets to you, after all these years."

"Sometimes."

He nodded. Maybe it was time to change the subject, even if only slightly. "So, are we looking for anyone in particular at this market?"

"Peter Garibaldi."

He glanced at Lina; she still stared out the window. "Did you say Garibaldi?"

"I did."

"Interesting," Reed said. "With the murder case I'm working, the name Garibaldi came up."

"You don't think it's a coincidence?"

"No."

"Doesn't that go against your famous rule?"

He nodded. "Very much so."

Chapter 11.

The party was somewhat muted, the clink of glass filled the fresco-covered walls of the bazaar, competing with impressively dull music – perhaps due to the early hour. The people within were a mixture of beard-oiling hipsters and more subdued artist types who seemed more on the ball without seeming to try, though for Reed's money, the occasional dangling cigarette spoiled the effect.

He glanced at his heavy coat and jeans... at least they were clean. Lina on the other hand, despite the chill to the air, was suddenly dressed appropriately in jacket, skirt and leggings – even her blue lips would have seemed like lipstick, rather than their actual shade.

"So, do you know what this Peter Garibaldi looks like?" Reed asked as they passed through the open doors.

"Huh?"

He lifted his voice a little. "Garibaldi – have you ever seen him?"

She gestured to a large poster on one of the white walls. A short fellow with greying, floppy-looking hair and thick-rimmed glasses stood shaking hands with a minister or a suit of some sort – it was a newspaper clipping, and the headline commemorated twenty years for owner Garibaldi at the Smith Street Bazaar. A quote alluded to his gratitude to the arts community for enabling him to stay open for so long, in a longstanding climate of uncertainty regarding arts funding.

"Ah. That should make it a little easier," Reed said.

"So, what's the plan?" she asked, eyes bright. "Let's pretend to be... an artist and his model! You can be the photographer because I have nicer legs."

"No."

Her lips verged toward a pout of blue but she snapped her fingers instead. "You're right. We can do better than that. How about this instead?" She slipped an arm around his waist. "I'm a Finnish actress and you're my scruffy arm-candy that I bring along to such parties to act as a buffer because I'm disgusted by the endless stream of vapid–"

"What about something simpler? I'm a patron of the arts and you're one of the many daughters of Death who can pass unseen through walls and rifle through anything in Garibaldi's office?"

"I think that's bending the rules, isn't it?"

"Indeed."

She folded her arms. "Fine. Leaving you to do what? Stroll around out here and moon over the art or the other models?"

"Other models? I thought you were an actress from Finland?"

"I went back," she said with a grin, before heading for the restrooms.

Reed sighed but at least she was proving to be more useful than the last few times they'd worked together... maybe she was more concerned than she seemed. He glanced around the room; abstract sculptures, paintings and light displays, long white tables laden with drinks and platters... and there, a hint of green.

Could be quieter at least.

He started toward the green, passing little groups of folks chatting over finger food, and found a pair of open sliding doors. Beyond, a comparatively quiet courtyard ringed by hanging potted plants and the large leaves of tropical plants. *A little retro. Maybe they're going for 'ironic'?*

A young couple were sitting together in one corner, kissing frantically enough for Reed to guess they were on coke or at least on *something*, but the pair stood and left without a word, the scent of their perfume and sweat mingling.

Odd.

In the corner he sat and tapped his foot on the stone.

In truth, he could have been doing a little more to help – he could have tried to find and speak to Garibaldi, find out a little more about the man's involvement but something had drawn him to the now-empty garden.

And it wasn't just a chance to think or the relative peace... he straightened.

The couple had left. *No-one* was in the garden now.

Strange for such a busy party.

Reed reached into his coat, gripping the handle of his gun. The music dimmed and the bazaar seemed to slow as the catering staff and their trays came to a halt, the patrons' mouths frozen in mid-sentence.

He shot to his feet, wheeling on the greenery.

"No need for that," a deep but weary voice announced from beyond the screen of plants.

Reed glared at the leaves, barrel trained on the point from where the words had issued. "You drew me here."

"Of course. It didn't seem necessary to interrupt their party; they're enjoying themselves, which is a rare thing for humans."

"You going to show yourself?"

A figure resolved from the green. A tall, barrel-chested man with a long black hair and a mighty beard; the figure wore a white toga and sandals but no sash. Instead, an image had been sewn onto the cloth – a mighty vine twisted around a tower of stone, more, the vine seemed to be *choking* the tower.

Green irises glowed from beneath a heavy brow but the figure did not inhabit the space fully; there was a faint transparency to him... which suggested a spirit rather than a god, though the sense of power was strong enough.

"Put away such items," the man instructed.

Reed lowered the gun; of course it would be useless but the silver bell on the other hand... He replaced his weapon but retrieved the bell while his hand was still within his coat, keeping it concealed in his palm.

"Who are you then?"

"Treveyos, leader of the Shining Leaves. And you are Reed Lavender, descended of Mors and just human enough to experience significant suffering in more ways than one should you choose to oppose our Restoration."

"Restoration of what?"

Treveyos smiled. "That you will see in time but tonight I bring you an offer and a promise."

"I imagine that's not as generous as it sounds."

"If you do not cease your efforts to thwart us then I promise you that we will 'finish with' Valen and take another of your family as a replacement," he said with an unpleasant smile. "However, if you stand aside now we will permit you and perhaps several of your choosing to survive the Restoration. The offer expires at the end of this conversation."

Reed stared at the man. Was he alive or dead? Spirit or projection? The name was certainly unfamiliar; surely he was no demi-god?

"Better for you if I do not have to wait, Lavender."

"And Valen is still whole? You can prove that?"

"Indeed."

"Then provide it and we can talk again."

He folded his arms, Gladiatorial biceps straining. "That is not part of my offer."

"Then you want me to take you at your word?"

"I swear it by Lady Feronia." The green in his eyes pulsed as he spoke.

Reed couldn't prevent a chill – was the Goddess truly helping Treveyos? Or was it all an elaborate ploy?

"Decide, little man."

"Let me ask you a question first. Do you actually believe we'll just give up? Let you keep Valen?"

"It is courteous to offer."

"Then you already knew my answer, before we spoke."

Treveyos inclined his head as he began to fade.

Chapter 12.

In the warm lamplight of his lounge, TV like a silent, blank face, Reed slouched into his old armchair, bowl of noodles resting on his chest. The scent of soy and lemon drifted up from his fork and his mouth watered.

"Is that all you can remember?" Max asked from the couch. His legs dangled over the arm rest and he stared up at the ceiling. Lina leant against the back of the couch, her silvery hair restless despite the lack of fan or air-con.

Reed took a bite, the flavour almost searing his tongue – good stuff. "Yes."

Lina sighed. "Let's not re-hash everything again."

"You're just saying that because you didn't find anything on Garibaldi," Max replied.

"Yet."

"Fine," Max said as he sat up. "What about this – why? That's been bugging me."

Reed nodded. "Me too. Why bother revealing himself to share his phony offer? It seems like more of an excuse to flex his muscles, so to speak. To taunt us."

"Typical behaviour of the egomaniac?," Max agreed.

"And if it truly was meant to be a genuine attempt to scare us off, doesn't the attempt suggest that the cultists *are* actually scared? Which, if you extend to its logical conclusion, doesn't line up with the kind of group that can capture and hold one of the family, let alone interest Feronia. It's something else."

Lina nodded. "I understand the taunting – it's exactly what I'd do to an enemy."

"What would Mother say about you, hearing you talk like that?" Max said.

"She'd be proud of me."

"Debatable."

"Shush, Brother." Lina began to pace, passing directly through the couch and coffee table as she did. "Was this Treveyos just trying to get a sense of who he and his pet humans were up against?"

"Maybe," Reed said. "It certainly wasn't an attack."

"I felt him leave the party, you know. He didn't seem as though he were someone like us... I think you were right about the projection."

"Mother said this was all Humans messing around," Max added.

Reed took another mouthful then set the bowl aside. "So, what now?"

A moment of silence and then Max shrugged. Lina had stopped pacing and she now stared across at him but said nothing.

"Waiting for me, I take it?"

Twin nods from his cousins.

Reed tapped a finger against the clean white of the bowl. "Why don't you both return to Aunty and get her advice. I'm going to follow up on the Garibaldi lead."

"Lost your impatience, all of a sudden?" Max asked.

"If Feronia really is involved I'm not too keen to go charging after them, no."

"Maybe it's for the best," Lina said. "We've been out here amongst the Living for a long time now."

Max stood with a sigh. "If you say so... but I think I can follow the trail to their lair, if you want me to risk it?"

"I'm still not sure we're ready to storm the castle."

"We can't wait forever either," Max said. "Valen is counting on us."

"I know."

His cousins blinked from view and Reed returned to his meal, chewing slowly now. Max and Lina were right. Valen might not be useful to the Shining Leaves forever... but it was madness to storm in blind. Mors would have some advice, surely. And in the meantime, Elise needed him.

When he finished, Reed took his bowl to the kitchen, rinsed it then started to fill up the sink with hot water and detergent. Steam soon fogged the window, revealing letters written by a small finger – Matthew.

He blinked, then gave a long sigh. "Sorry, Lily, I haven't forgotten you."

Even so, his legs were heavy and he found himself blinking a lot as he worked, frequent yawns stretching his jaw. *Call it a night, already.*

He did, drawn down by sleep swiftly and only waking to the merry sound of a bandsaw. He groaned, squinting at the alarm clock, nine in the morning. "Better, but still most unwelcome, Steve."

Still, he stumbled his way through a shower, then a breakfast of fruit and yogurt, and only when he found his phone – flat – and plugged it in to call Duong, did he really begin to feel awake.

"Where the hell have you been?" the detective asked.

"Sleeping. And I hope that isn't suddenly a crime."

"Clever. I've sent someone around – I've got something for you and we've just picked up a guy too. Thought you'd want to see the interview."

"You caught Elise's killer?"

"Veronica's, probably," he said. "And I could do without the surprise in your voice, you know."

"You're in a bit of a mood."

"I quit smoking last night," he said. "Be ready."

The line went dead.

"Hmmm." Reed nearly dialled again – who knew how far away the squad car was – but Duong probably wouldn't answer. *And if he does, I don't know if I want to hear what he has to say.* It was the fourth time the man had tried to quit and each attempt had resulted in enough tension to string a harp.

For complete weeks at a time.

Good on him for trying again at least.

Reed waited in the lobby, searching Google for any reference to Treveyos while he paced. Nothing came up and the only reference to 'Shining Leaves' was a sludge metal band from Louisiana; their Facebook page boasting a foreboding shot of the wetlands at dusk for an album cover. "Should probably check them out," he murmured.

When the white and blue of a squad car pulled up before the apartment building, Reed strode out to greet the officer, breath steaming in the chill morning. From inside the car, he glanced up at the empty branches shuddering their final leaves in the rising wind.

"You're Lavender, right? The private investigator? You've worked with the boss a few times, right?" The man was a little younger, his blue shirt bearing the badge of a Constable: Huggins. Not unfamiliar precisely, but neither could Reed place him at a particular crime scene or interview.

"Looking to hire me?" Reed asked.

"Actually... maybe." The man's tone wavered, uncertainty clear.

"I can be discreet," Reed said as he straightened in his seat.

Huggins tapped his fingers on the steering wheel. "It'd have to be, I suppose... I, you know what? I shouldn't even ask you. It might put you in an uncomfortable position."

"Why?"

"Shit. Forget I said anything, I'm just being stupid."

"I'm not going to give you a hard time, if that's what you're worried about," Reed said. "I've taken all kinds of cases over the years."

Huggins didn't answer at first.

Reed removed a little notebook, since his phone was nearly flat, and a pen. "Sure I can't help?"

"I don't know," he said. "I kind of volunteered to pick you up because I wanted to ask you but now that you're here... shit."

Reed waited.

After a time, Huggins sighed, glancing at Reed once again before returning his gaze to the road. "You must get a bit of work from paranoid boyfriends and husbands, right? Nothing new there, I bet?"

"Not really. But then, they're not always paranoid."

"Hmmm."

"You have someone in mind? Girlfriend?"

"Fiancée."

"But you've got doubts."

"Now that we're thinking of getting married... I guess I do." He shrugged. "I mean, in a way I wouldn't be surprised. We both cheated on our exes – it's how we met. Another old story, right?"

"What makes you think she's cheating?"

He shrugged. "I dunno. She's been a bit distant. A bit secretive, maybe – won't let me touch her phone. Last few times we've tried to go out on the weekend she's been busy with the girls. Not much to go on, is it?"

Reed made a few notes. "I can follow her and see where she ends up if you want but what makes you say taking the job might make things uncomfortable for me?"

"Ah, because I think I know who she's seeing."

"Someone I know?"

"Yeah. Detective Duong."

Chapter 13.

Innocuous cream-coloured walls coated the interrogation room in a sense of the blank, of the regular – nothing like in the movies, of course. And the dullness of it all was almost disconcerting; an outdated video camera set up in the corner, a pasty-looking thug sitting across from Duong. It was almost a cliché. Even the suspect's fingers twitched as the constant fast tap of his shoes filled the space while Duong and his partner waited for an answer.

"Trevor." Duong's voice was soft.

Trevor blinked, eyes a little wide but a grin stretched across his face, teeth clenched. Once, he might have been a good-looking guy. Once. "Told you already, cop. She wasn't supposed to get hurt."

"Sure, that I can understand. Accidents are called accidents for a reason. Can you tell us how it happened?"

"What about a cigarette?"

"Later," Duong's partner said, his deep frown adding to a rather brutish look. Phillips was his name.

"Fine," the suspect said. He leant back, scratching

himself through his ancient Motley Crue t-shirt. "I broke in and she found me. I wanted her laptop and a few other things. Gave her a shove and she fell down – no way that killed her though, right?"

"What do you mean?" Duong asked, leaning across the table.

"I heard it was poison."

"Where'd you hear that?" Phillips demanded.

Trevor snickered. "Word gets round, come on."

"You know we have your prints in Miss Hannington's kitchen and her bedroom. We have over a dozen calls within forty-eight hours between the two of you and evidence of crack in her bloodstream – you're a known dealer, Trevor. She was using or pushing or both and it seems pretty clear you gave her an overdose," Duong said. "What we'd like to know is why? She holding back on you?"

"Nope. Nothing like that."

"Then what was it like?" Phillips asked.

Trevor shrugged and the tapping of his feet grew a little more frantic. "You ever gonna get me that cigarette like you promised?"

Reed frowned. Maybe Veronica wasn't dealing, maybe she wasn't skimming profits or whatever, maybe... he leaned closer to the screen. Was it more personal? Hadn't there been something at her place – the toys! He straightened, turning to Huggins.

"I need to speak with Duong. I think I know what this guy's hiding."

Huggins raised an eyebrow but slipped from the surveillance room with a nod, leaving Reed to pace before the screen. Huggins's revelation and request had hung in the air between them for a while but for now, Veronica's death and any connection to Elise had to come first.

Still, what was Duong doing, messing with one of his men?

On the screen, Duong told Trevor to think about his answer then opened the door, Huggins remaining mostly unseen. Then the Detective nodded to Phillips and a moment later, joined Reed in the surveillance room.

"Let's hear it, Reed." Duong said. His expression was one of weariness and the stubble on his cheeks was long. Huggins stood nearby, expression offering no hint of the man's suspicions.

"I think it's about custody," Reed said. "Remember at the house? The toys and the empty kid's room? That's why he's not fazed by the questions around drugs – we're way off there."

Duong shook his head. "Reed, we knew that."

Reed blinked.

"Yeah. There's an AVO out on him and a long history of domestic violence. We've got this, okay? If you want to help then go and follow-up with the landlord. I'll email you the details; that's mostly what I wanted your help with anyway.'

"Right, yeah, sorry," Reed said, clearing his throat. *Shit, am I just as tired too? Should've trusted him to have all that figured out already.*

"Huggins can take you back to your place if you want – but either way, I expect anything you get to come to me right away."

"Right."

Back in the police cruiser, Reed skimmed the email on

his phone – then his eyes widened.

The landlord bore a rather familiar name.

Robert Garibaldi. "Hmmm." The man seemed like a dedicated property manager and maybe he truly was so incredibly busy with his galleries and boutiques that he'd not been able to find time to speak with Duong or another officer, but a surprise visit was always a good choice.

Maybe Garibaldi would be off-balance enough to reveal *something* at least. According to the email, the fellow had been renting Veronica's place privately, bypassing the usual estate agent arrangement. Which didn't necessarily mean anything dodgy but he was a potential source of valuable information at least.

"So, have you had a chance to think about helping me?" Huggins asked.

Reed glanced up from his phone; the officer had his eyes on the traffic. "I have... and I'll keep my eyes open but I have to say this, I say it to everyone, but sometimes people don't like what I discover. Think you're ready for either outcome?"

He nodded.

Reed exhaled. "All right, I'm going to ring Garibaldi's offices and then we can talk about my fee."

***

An exceedingly competent receptionist arranged a meeting with Garibaldi for the afternoon; the minor mogul would be inspecting a property in the outer suburbs, a leafy part of Pakenham. Quite convenient perhaps, and refreshingly accommodating, considering the man had been fobbing off the police. The obvious question was *why* Garibaldi was suddenly so willing to meet – was he just trying to get it over with because he truly was that busy, or was it something else?

Did the man think it was easier than talking to the police?

Or was it something else?

Pakenham was a little over an hour's drive but Reed arrived early enough to park up the street from the mansion and wait for Garibaldi.

Once in place, he flicked the radio on and slumped down in his seat, phone in one hand, occasionally glancing at the image onscreen. Garibaldi resembled his poster from Smith Street; grey hair, short, clean-shaven... typical businessman look, really. But was he more than that? Reed glanced up at the flash of light – a silver Subaru had pulled up before the house.

"Time to find out."

He reached into the glove box to remove his gun without taking his gaze from the house.

A grey-haired man, Garibaldi himself, circled to the boot, opened it and rummaged around. He soon pulled free a roll of carpet then started up the path. Reed raised an eyebrow. It was a quiet street, sure enough, but if the man was preparing for a murder with that carpet, why not hide it better?

You're just being paranoid.

After all, Garibaldi was looking at the place, probably as an investment and maybe that meant a renovation? Despite the nice exterior, it might have been hideous inside, bare floors everywhere.

In and of itself? Hardly an unusual thing for someone in real estate to do.

Yet there were too many unpleasant coincidences around the man for everything to be innocent. And of course, there was the tendency for the rich to pay people to do the things they couldn't be bothered with.

"Reed, I wouldn't go in there after him."

He flinched.

Lina sat in the backseat, arms folded.

Reed sighed, hanging his head a moment, letting the thunder in his veins ease. "Can't you warn me somehow? We all had deal, you know, years and years ago. You'd call first, remember?"

She snickered. "That was boring."

"My heart doesn't think so."

"Don't be ridiculous – you aren't going to die in this car, trust me."

He twisted in his seat. "Don't tell me about the future."

"It's not a promise. Just a feeling."

"Good... I suppose."

"It is. Think about it," she said with a smile. "If you want to live forever, logically, you just have to stay in this car."

"Well, I'm not planning on that." His life had already been extended far beyond its natural means thanks to his 'gift' but that meant collecting all the guilt that came with the time he stole, as it piled up before him. *Other people's days whether I want them or not – Dad never did explain that part before he disappeared.*

"Then head in there alone and you might die early," Lina said.

"Why?"

"Can't you feel it?"

"Obviously I'm not as finely-tuned as you."

"He's planning a Summoning and he's looking for flesh."

"Shit." Reed straightened. "I thought he'd *maybe* be a lead in the case, you know, just boring little things like drug dealing and murder."

"He can be both."

Reed straightened, reaching for the door handle. "Then I'm going to stop him."

"Dangerous."

"Fine, what did Aunty say? Is that why you're here?"

"Partly." Lina stretched her legs beneath his seat, kicking at him with an idleness he did his best to ignore while she spoke. "She said it's still up to us – delivered the words with a pretty stoic expression, too."

"Very funny."

"I'm saving some better jokes for later," she admitted. "But she did ask me to remind you that you're certainly welcome to bend a few rules."

"That's not comforting."

"It should be; I wish I was the beneficiary of such largesse."

"She's telling me I'm free to kill."

"I know that."

"Well it doesn't mean I'd be free of consequences as they occur on the human side of the Fringe."

"You can be sure that anyone working for Treveyos will be bending every rule out there."

"Hmmm." The gun was heavy in his grip. "Did she say anything else?"

"Yes. She wants someone a little more 'considered' than just Max and I – which, when it comes to Mother, was her way of saying she thinks we're immature."

"Meaning?"

"Meaning that Max is bringing Potter along."

"Perfect."

Chapter 14.

Night had fallen then worn down to midnight, a beaming moon spilling across the street. The light gleamed on letterboxes and windscreens alike, half a dozen clouds milling about above but not a single one of them willing to even approach the giant orb where it cast a cool, even dispassionate eye upon the suburb.

Yet Max had arrived, bringing Potter with him.

While Max was attired in his regular get up, Potter was something of a traditionalist – a long trench coat of black and a shaven head, pale skin bright. The man even bore a scythe that dripped frost-bitten soil as he stood, staring from heavy brows at the mansion with an expression of great distaste.

"Shouldn't we stop Garibaldi now?" Reed asked the man.

Potter did not answer; he didn't even turn his head.

"If we let him half-complete the Summoning and interrupt it, we have a better chance of dealing with the demon too," Max said.

"Correct, Maximilian," Potter replied.

Reed folded his arms, even as he nodded – they were

right, though it didn't change the fact that Potter was still being a prick. "Let me know when you're ready then." He started for the car, opening the door and slumping in the driver's seat where he reached for his water bottle, taking a long drink.

Max blinked into the passenger seat. "You still don't like him very much, do you?"

"Nope."

"Come on, Reed. He saved your life, doesn't that count for–"

"Nothing at all." He glanced out the window to where Lina had started to skip around Potter, pausing every now and then to pluck a silver hair from her head, raise it to her lips and blow it toward him.

Each strand twisted on her breath, spinning up to land on his neck or check, his head and face and even some upon his hands. There, each one slipped beneath Potter's skin and glowed, almost like veins.

Potter bore the Strengthening Ritual without comment – though Reed was sure the man would have wanted her to stop skipping around as she worked. Still, it was another sign that everyone was taking the Summoning *very* seriously.

"Reed, you still with us?"

"Yeah. Look, if this is such a big deal, who else is going to be in there? Garibaldi won't be alone, surely?"

"We can't tell," Max said. "Half the cult could be in there or only Garibaldi himself, taking some godsforsaken foolish risk. Either way, him agreeing to your meeting is probably a trap."

"Hmmm."

"What?"

"I know it's probably a trap and I'm just as keen as you to spring it and get some answers but it's just that I'm feeling a little outgunned – even more than before."

Max put a cold hand on Reed's shoulder. "We need you, you know that."

"I know you need me for when you've overstayed your welcome on this side but what if he's summoning a Lich Lord or something? They like me even less than Potter – that's not something I can handle alone."

"It might just be a First Echelon Demon for all we know," Max said.

"They can be trouble enough."

Max snorted. "You really want to see this as all bad, don't you, cousin? Look, if it was something truly catastrophic, do you think Mother – not to mention the others, would leave it to us?"

"No, but I think everyone in our odd little family has differing ideas about exactly what amounts to 'catastrophic' and that's always been troubling too."

A crimson light flashed across Max's sunglasses.

His head snapped around to the mansion, where a red glow flared in a top floor window, quickly fading. "Here we go then."

"Hurry it along, human," Potter's voice boomed from outside.

Reed ground his teeth as he exited the car and broke into a run, where he caught up with the other three. He leapt over a small row of shrubs, the others simply passing through, and paused at the front door, which stood ajar. *Garibaldi definitely wants an audience.*

"How are we doing this?" Reed asked.

"Break down the door; it's one of the bedrooms," Potter said and as usual, there was a sense that he was simply speaking some words aloud, rather than directing them *to* Reed. "At the same time, we will break the spectral wards and outflank the human."

Before Reed could answer Potter had disappeared.

Lina grinned at him before following suit.

"Try not to worry, we've done this sort of thing before, remember?" Max said.

"That's *exactly* what worries me."

"It wasn't that bad."

"Two buildings burned down and I was nearly cut in half. Chris had to be brought back from Pluto's Sleeping Chambers. It cost Aunty some pretty serious favours too."

"Well, Christina is fine now and she's actually speaking to me again so that's something," Max replied. "And more importantly, we stopped that cloven... thing from getting out. This won't be like that; Potter's here."

"You're probably right." Potter *would* make a difference. Second eldest, much favoured, powerfully decisive. *And of course, he won't thank any of us afterward.*

Max disappeared but his voice lingered. "See you in there."

Reed exhaled as he drew his gun, clicked the safety off and then reached for his silver bell – the Sonorous. He muffled the clapper then nudged the door open with his foot, striding within. A darkened entryway bore a coat rack and hall table, marbled floors clacking beneath his feet. Open curtains let scant moonlight in but his night vision exceeded the average person even without the lunar aid.

A narrow staircase led up and around the wall, to a

balcony and a row of closed doors with ornate gold handles. The mere whisper of a red glow came from beneath the hallway to the end of the balcony – somewhere beyond would wait the door to a bedroom and Garibaldi, along with whatever else he had summoned.

Reed squeezed the grip of his gun, then started up the stairs, pulse racing now.

The fear was irrational in a way, dying would 'only' change him but his human side seethed with the desire to cling to life, to avoid risk, to turn back toward safety – utterly unremarkable reaction, really. *What's irrational is thinking safety even exists.*

At the top, he slowed enough to listen, but no sounds filled the house, just his own breathing. Just what was Garibaldi calling? Anything from the first few Echelons would be something they could hopefully manage. Anything lower...

In the hallway the red glow grew, though it rose and fell as Reed neared the door and now, a sibilance seemed to escape from beyond. But still no words, no true sound that he recognised. *Like a hallucination for the ears.* A tingling spread across his skin too, warmth coming with it – and there were no central heating ducts in the hall.

"Ready, boots?" Reed murmured.

He lifted a knee and kicked.

Wood splintered with a mighty crack. Shock ran up his calf and he grunted as he half-charged, half-stumbled into a red room, weapons raised.

Garibaldi knelt on carpet before what appeared to be a chest-high anthill on the floorboards, dark earth trickling down the side of the peaked form. It pulsed with the red glow. The room was bare save for what rested before Reed, and he raised the gun with a frown. Garibaldi hadn't turned at the intrusion.

"Get away from that," Reed snapped. He glanced around the room – no sign of the others.

"I cannot!" The reply came as a shriek and still the fellow did not turn.

Reed approached, slowly. "If you think whatever you're summoning will spare you, then you're wrong."

A groan.

Reed kept the gun trained on Garibaldi, shifting to get a better view of the mound, even as he raised his voice. "Max? Lina?"

The ant-hill, if it truly was one, trembled.

"Last chance, buddy."

Garibaldi twitched and still gave no answer – but Reed kept his distance, circling the mound until he could see Garibaldi's face – and flinched.

The man had rent his own cheeks with his nails, they were red-tipped where his hands hung before him and his eyes were rolling, blinking furiously. *Shit, is* he *the sacrifice?* Reed stepped forward –

Earth exploded.

He threw an arm up as he fell into a crouch. Wet, pungent dirt splattered across him. He stood, spitting as he did, only to fall back.

Garibaldi was gone. All that remained was a splash of blood upon the piece of carpet. And hulking above Reed now, stooped beneath the roof, stood a glistening creature of scales and elongated limbs. Heat pumped forth as it moved, filling the room with muggy, heavy air too. Its single eye, near the size of Reed's head, glowed red as it peered down at him. The thing took a step forward, a sucking mud sound following, and scales fell. They were black, yet seemed polished to a high sheen – or was it the gleam of condensation?

Tri-claws ended each limb and the slender body curled along one wall, not spider-like so much as a shifting, rippling change occurring as it moved. Reed gave more ground. The eye followed him, light intensifying.

He fired.

The shot cracked through the air – ricocheting off the creature.

And having no effect.

"Idiot," Reed shouted at himself. Whatever it was, First or Twelfth Echelon demon, it had to be stopped. He lifted the Sonorous and snapped his wrist, the silver bell pealing once, then twice, three times as he skipped back. The demon shrank away, raising multiple limbs to cover its head.

Reed rang the bell again. He raised his voice. "In the name of Mors I command you, Return!"

It did not fade or shrink or disappear. No colour leeched from the thing, as if it were being banished beyond the Fringe, as it should have. The summoned creature was stronger than the Sonorous, and while Reed's bell was by no means one of the five Greater Bells, his old friend was no wind chime either.

And so he did not stop the ringing.

"Reed!" Max appeared before him, sunglasses gone, eyes wide. "You have to help us."

"What?" Reed looked back and forth from creature to

cousin. "What about this thing?"

Max caught his arm, with barely a glance at the thing cringing in the corner of the room. "They're trying to take Potter."

"Who?"

"We have to hurry. Lina's already exhausted – she had to Return."

"But what about that?" Reed pointed with his gun.

"Let it go – it's only a Scale Fiend, it'll feed for a while and then slink back to the Underworld; its time is limited here."

"Feed?"

Max's expression grew desperate. "Trust me; we can't waste any more time. It was a trap like we thought, but just not the one we imagined."

"Fool!" a new voice cried. "You mean to leave this thing here?"

Reed spun.

A woman stood nearby, dark hair tied back into a wreath. She wore a brown tunic and bare feet, and carried a longbow as tall as she herself. The bow gave off its own light, a faint silver. Her eyes blazed a vivid blue as they bored into? Max, who pointed back at her.

"You don't understand, Adrina."

"I do understand – and I know your mother would not wish for you to permit a beast like this to terrorise the Humans." To Reed she said, "Do keep ringing your bell."

He turned back to the Scale Fiend. It had risen again, shoulders brushing the roof, head leaning forward.

Reed rang the Sonorous once more, the clear note driving the demon back.

A blazing white arrow flew by his head, striking the thing directly in the chest. It writhed, but another arrow followed. This one plunged into the neck, pinning the creature down. Adrina strode forward, lifted another arrow and drew the full span of the bow and let loose.

Blood sprayed as the eye exploded.

The demon grew still.

Adrina turned back to them, an expression of distaste clear beneath flecks of blood. "Thank you, Reed Lavender."

Chapter 15.

"Thanks. We appreciate the help," Reed said as he exhaled, lowering his weapons. "Ah, have we met before?"

"She's one of Diana's kids," Max said. "And we have to go."

He looked back to Adrina. "Your mother is The Huntress?"

"Yes," she replied with a short nod. "And thanks to your aid, I shall now help rescue old Potter now."

"How generous," Max said, winking out of sight.

Adrina followed in kind, leaving Reed alone with the scent of damp earth and something acrid, but the Fiend was already gone. He shook his head, even as he charged into the hall. What could have driven Garibaldi to do such a thing? Did he know he was going to die?

Was he a cultist or a pawn?

Outside, a dozen figures in white robes had Potter surrounded. He thrashed against unseen bonds, the silver strands beneath his skin flaring. The men and women of the Shining Leaves were chanting in unison, broken Latin phrases. Yet it seemed the tall Fasces each carried, all raised high, were the things holding actually Potter in place. Max was calling for his brother and Adrina stood beside him, an arrow nocked.

"What now?" Reed asked. He could shoot them himself, or at least, a fair few and stop the ritual, but despite Aunty's 'permission' being granted, it still didn't grant him a free pass when it came to murder.

"It will just take one to break the circle," Adrina said. "And I could burn one of the Fasces with my arrow but that may constitute a rule broken. I am not clear on my duty as I did not expect to see surrogates of Feronia here."

Max wheeled on her, mouth open – only to fade into nothingness.

Too long on the human side.

And worse, Max wouldn't be able to return soon enough to make a difference. "We have to do something – these people have no just cause," Reed said.

"Just? That is not for me to decide."

Reed clenched his jaw. "They already have Valen."

Now she frowned, her bright eyes dimming somewhat. "That is not normal."

"Will you help?"

She lifted her weapon, drew a bead and then paused, lowering the bow once more. "No, I do not think so. Even with what you have said, they are not beasts like the Fiend. I could not raise a hand against those chosen by Feronia."

"I'm not sure I agree about humans not being beasts."

She smiled faintly. "Though we have not met before tonight, Reed Lavender, I sense a certain quality within you. You know what do to; simply break one of the Fasces."

And then she was gone, leaving him standing in the night on the lawn before the mansion, mere metres away from a group of people oblivious to him as they struggled to ensnare Potter.

Reed glanced around the darkened houses. The gun wasn't precisely out of the question... was it? A single shot to startle them? Occupied houses were some distance away. Just how much attention would it bring down? So far, it was a miracle that a passerby or resident hadn't come to investigate. Were the cultists doing something to cloak their activities?

"Shit."

No need to kill them – just disrupt it. And maybe take some Time from one, give them a good shock. *And maybe don't rule out using the gun either.*

Reed wheeled, scanning the street. Garibaldi's car... the boot was still open. He glanced at Potter, whose expression was caught between rage and pain, then charged the car. "Come on," he muttered.

There had to be something!

Reed tore at the mat in the boot, revealing the spare tyre... and the tyre iron. "Perfect."

He snatched it free.

The chanting rose, tempo increasing. A roar answered the voices – Potter had fallen to his knees. Reed sprinted for the nearest cultist, leaping at the man, iron raised, and swung at the Fasces.

A thunderclap split the air.

Reed crashed to the grass. The thump hurt his hip but a jolt ran up his arm – instantly eclipsing other pain. His hand contracted into a claw. The tyre iron was nowhere to be seen. Not a single cultist had even turned, confident no doubt in their unseen barrier.

Which ruled out the gun.

Reed swore as he climbed to his knees. Potter was

trembling now, head bowed and the silvery strands of Lina's hair dim. His scythe lay beside him, out of reach.

Think, idiot, think.

The Sonorous!

Reed tore the bell from his jacket pocket and swung it, a sweet, clear note ringing out in the night.

Potter did not move but his form grew immediately transparent – and the chanting faltered. Reed stepped closer, flicking his wrist once more, and the Sonorous sang again, banishing Potter beyond the Fringe.

Saved.

Silence followed, broken only by Reed's breathing.

And then the Fasces began to lower. The white-robed figures turned on him; hoods cast low, revealing frowning mouths only. One man took a step forward and Reed raised his gun, levelling it at his chest.

"Leave."

The figure hesitated. Others moved up to flank him, one woman and a man with a grey beard cut close.

"Your interference tonight will not be forgotten," greybeard said.

Reed moved the gun to the speaker.

As one, the robes collapsed, as if a great, silent wind had sucked the people out from the clothing. Each Fasces fell too, and just as swiftly, the grass rose, twisting and turning as it claimed both wood and cloth, a sweet, springtime smell left in their place.

Chapter 16.

The twenty-four-hour petrol station glowed green as Reed pulled into a park and cut the engine. A hulking truck was the only other vehicle at the station, the bearded driver tapping his boot as he filled up. The green glinted on the chrome of the tanker.

Reed sighed and leant back in the seat. Getting out seemed far too great a task; his limbs had grown heavy and his stomach writhed. His lips were dry and so obviously food and drink were in order, but a storm of questions had to be answered first – or at least, attempted.

Back at the Garibaldi property he'd checked the hungry grass for remains of the cultists and their materials but found nothing, and so returned to his car then drove a highway almost empty of traffic, trying to put it all together.

But satisfactory answers had eluded him.

Max and Lina were safe, that much was certain. Potter would be well enough, despite being banished by the bell. In any other circumstance, the Sonorous wouldn't have been strong enough, but weakened and under threat as he was, even an old hand like Potter couldn't resist.

Reed did find a tiny smile at the thought. "He'll hate being in my debt."

But how had the cultists sprung their trap? And when was the trap set up – after Treveyos appeared in the garden? Just why had Garibaldi gone along with it all? And if the man was able to summon a Scale Fiend, just what else could be brought forth? *And those twelve were by no means tiptoeing acolytes.*

As suspected, Reed had been bait rather than the main target – Garibaldi used him to ensure more of Death's children came along.

At least it explained a little more of *how* they'd been able to capture Valen.

Still, someone had to have helped the Shining Leaves in the first place. The question was who? An agent or child of the gods? *That's not something I want to confront right now.* And who was Treveyos exactly? The beneficiary of such help... or something more powerful? If he was only human, it seemed he'd found a way to blackmail a Goddess. Reed shook his head – no, that was an assumption. It was possible she was *willingly* aiding them for some reason; a troubling thought, that one. Even Adrina had been hesitant to interfere – though that was typical of the children of gods and supposedly Diana and Feronia were on good terms.

Only one person could truly provide answers now.

Aunty.

Reed climbed out of the car, moving only slowly, flexing his still-tingling hand as he approached the bathroom. He nudged the door open with his boot and the auto-light flicked on. He raised his eyebrows at the not-unclean image that confronted him. "Seen worse."

The white-tiled floor had a few footprints and the stall was beyond scuffed but at least the sink had been manufactured in the current century. He turned the squeaking taps and half-filled the basin, then fished out a coin – this time a five cent piece.

It plopped into the water and sank to the bottom.

"With this token I call upon Mors," he said. "Let her hear my mortal voice; a whisper across water."

A chill filled the bathroom, prickling the hairs along his neck and forearms.

His breath steamed as he turned; Aunty stood in her endlessly black robe, her silver shawl tied as a bonnet this time. A skull seemed to grin at him from the depths, though that was hardly her manner – the idea of Aunty grinning, let alone smiling, was odd to say the least. Her flowing black hair was hidden this time and as ever, while vague hints of her true face appeared, he saw only bone.

The fluorescent light buzzed out.

"Nephew."

"Aunty, I need your help," he said, her form still easy to see thanks to his 'gifts'.

"It is forbidden."

He sighed. "No, I mean, I need answers. I imagine Max or Lina told you what happened?"

"I have been kept abreast of things, yes," she said. "They are dutiful children, I am quite fortunate, don't you agree?"

"Very much so," he said, holding back a sigh. "I wanted to ask about the cult and Feronia – what can you tell me?"

"Little, I fear. Feronia has been... sulking for eons now. I wonder if she hasn't started another temper tantrum."

Reed swallowed. "Tantrum?"

She shrugged her bony shoulders. "It happens – humans usually consider them natural disasters, though more than enough are certainly just that and that alone."

"And that's who you want me to rescue Valen from?"

"So it would seem. Feronia is no doubt still upset at the way cities have long been encroaching upon her domain. I have asked Diana to reach out to her."

"And in the meantime?"

"I want my son returned, Reed," she said, her flat voice boring into him, not louder, not any more infused with emotion, just... undeniable – as though not only his ears, but his whole body had been compelled to listen. "And Max and Lina will curtail their movements when you close with these 'Shining Leaves' in the future, as I do not wish to put them in any more danger."

Damn. Understandable, but... damn. "And Potter?"

"*All* children."

"Then are we on the right path – is Emerald the place I need to go?"

"Yes."

He hesitated.

"Reed?"

There were so many questions to ask and many seemed to linger at the very edge of his awareness but he couldn't bring them forth; the weight of being pitted against a Goddess was like a vice. "Can I ask for a favour?"

"Perhaps."

"I need your Mark."

"Why so?"

"Because I feel I'm going to have to use the Fringe on my way to Emerald and my human side always draws too much attention."

"Your flesh."

"Yes, my flesh, Aunty. Will you help? It'll bring Valen back faster."

"Hmmm. Your embarrassingly unsubtle attempt to sway me aside, the notion is not without merit." She straightened. "Be still a moment." A bony hand rose and hovered before his chest and the cold intensified as she sketched a symbol in the air; it blazed black, vaguely like a hangman's rope, and then disappeared.

"Thank you." Now, if any of the various dread creatures that lived in the Fringe were drawn to his body, they'd encounter Death's mark and know he was off-limits. *Which should do the trick for* most *of them.*

"Now go, attend to your duties, Reed."

She was gone and he leant against the basin a moment. "Of course, but what now?"

He hadn't received as many answers as he'd have liked, typical of Aunty, but those he'd managed to glean were troubling enough. A possible tantrum by a Goddess that would likely lead to a natural disaster. *Wonderful.*

Back in the petrol station he ordered dim sims and potato cakes, and took one of the hard, plastic seats and chewed through the 'meal', not really tasting a single bite but the hot, greasy food somehow satisfying enough.

Heading to Emerald alone wasn't much of an idea. Max and Lina would help – to a point, and then he was by himself unless he wanted to risk Aunty's wrath, which wasn't a good idea. Duong and the police would only useful up to a point – there was no way they'd survive the Fringe, let alone *believe* in any of it. But there was someone he could ask, someone who might help... maybe, if she wasn't too upset with him.

Chapter 17.

Sleep was a vague sketch of rest – no more than that, and he dragged himself from bed with much grumbling when the roar of his mobile phone echoed from the kitchen. The blanket had fallen aside, like a crime that left his skin exposed to the chill air and he snarled at it as he squinted against the brightness of the room. *Shit, what time is it?*

He fumbled across the bench to snatch up the phone and answer the call.

"Yeah, hello – this is Reed Lavender speaking."

"Mr Lavender, I'm so glad I got onto you before I left. It's Irene Roberts."

Damn, I've got nothing. "Irene, I'm sorry I haven't been in touch."

"God has his own timetable, son. I understand and I know you'll call me when you find the truth, but I'm needed back home and I feel I've worn out my welcome with my cousin."

"I will call you as soon as I can," he said. "I promise."

She thanked him and hung up, the weariness in her voice clear.

Reed tapped his fingers on the bench, staring into the clump of dirty dishes in the sink without really seeing them. He'd neglected Elise again... even with the apparent link between the two problems. *I should have found something on Garibaldi, if he was directly involved. And even if he wasn't; he was still my best lead.*

He lifted his mobile and called Duong. No answer.

Yet almost right after he put the phone back down, it rang: Detective Duong.

"I've got some news you might want," Reed said when he answered.

"Let me guess, Lavender," he said. "Garibaldi's disappeared?"

Close enough. "Right – I found his car in Pakenham and some odd things in one of his properties."

"So did we," Duong said. "A mound of dirt on the floorboards and claw marks on the floor and walls being the strangest of the discoveries, aside from the blood. And thanks for calling me about it now, half a day later."

"I'm juggling a few things right now."

"Yeah, yeah. So, what did you make of it all, then?"

"No idea – you know what arty folks are like," Reed said. "I assumed that was what was going on."

"Yeah, maybe. And the car?"

"Ah..."

"Reed. Did you even search it?" He sighed. "What's going on, I thought you'd be all over me with questions by now."

"Something came up."

"Meaning?"

"Family shit – maybe I'll bore you with the details later,"

he said after a moment's hesitation, hoping it'd be enough. "What did I miss?"

"All right. No surprise here but Peter Garibaldi was a member at Bay City Golf Club. We got another name from Veronica's ex – another club member and likely the distributor for both of them. Alan Dunstall; ostensibly he runs a restaurant but we're pretty sure he's the one we're looking for."

"And you found this out from the car?"

"There were quite a few interesting documents jammed into a briefcase, along with another suitcase of clothes and a laptop."

Just where did the man think he was going after summoning that thing? "But he didn't take any of it."

"No, so he was either forced to run without any of it or he's dead. Maybe Dunstall is cleaning house, maybe we're getting too close for him."

"Could be... but anyone paid to kill Garibaldi wouldn't have left that stuff behind, how clear does it make the link between them?"

"Not very – you have to put it with what Trevor said, to be honest," he replied. "Maybe the killer was interrupted, maybe he didn't realise what was in the car, there's too much we don't know right now."

"So have you spoken to this Dunstall yet?"

"Holidaying in Malaysia."

"Risky."

"Right. It's likely his supply *is* coming from somewhere in Southeast Asia but I'm not jumping the gun; still, we've already been referred to his legal representation."

"So you're going after his dealers in the meantime?"

"Right."

Reed started to pace. Joining Duong now would likely offer new leads on Elise's killer but Valen was in greater danger... he swallowed an oath. *I need to be in two places at once. Or better, I need one of my cousins.* "I'd really like to help but I have to take care of something first. Keep me in the loop."

"Only if you do another favour for me – and you owe me, remember?"

"Right."

"Drop that thing with Huggins."

Reed stopped.

"What?"

"Lavender, I'm serious. What's happening between me and Lucy is none of your business and Huggins is just going to have to deal with it. She's made her choice."

"What?"

"And don't tell him we've spoken. I've got enough on my plate right now, just conclude your investigation without finding anything, right?"

"That's not how I work."

"Well it's going to have to be this time."

"So she's already told him, is that what you're saying?"

"She's not ready."

Reed scratched at the stubble on his cheek. "I don't like this at all."

"That makes two of us, Lavender, but I'm not going to push her. It's not my place."

"Maybe you should."

"Maybe you should stay out of it, like I asked," Duong said.

The line went dead.

"Shit." Reed resumed pacing. Had Huggins let something slip? Or was it just a lucky guess – maybe Lucy mentioned something about Huggins; maybe Duong had found his fellow officer's willingness to act as chauffeur for Reed somewhat suspicious? Maybe he'd picked up something from the hotel?

Either way, things were shaping up into a fine mess.

And yet, it still had to be set aside for now – Reed had other calls to make, and the first wasn't necessarily going to be any easier than contacting Huggins, unless some ground work happened first.

Time to get some help.

He grabbed his laptop, then the stereo remote and hit play, before slumping into the armchair where he started searches on Lily and Matthew Stephens while Elvis Costello's *Armed Forces* rang out.

On Facebook he found a likely candidate right away, clicked through some pictures and there, a memorial image of Lily from a few years back, her cheeks dimpled by a smile. So, the correct Stephens. Without too much trouble he had a suburb and then, via directory assistance, a phone number.

Social networking makes it all far too easy sometimes.

The next steps would have to wait but if he was lucky, he'd be able to combine some of them with Valen's rescue. He just had to collect a few things and then, off to the nearest cemetery where hopefully, Lily would hear him out.

Chapter 18.

Reed ran the bath.

Once the water was not only warm but high enough for submersion, he upended a little bottle of Frankincense oil into the bath then stripped down. He dipped a foot into the water, then the rest of his body and let the warmth and the scent soothe him, sucking in a deep breath. More important than the comfort it offered, his efforts acted as a base deterrent for spirits, ghouls and Sneaks.

Next, he rubbed Amber Oil into his skin to help shield it from decay, a woody scent joining the others, and finally stood with a sigh – drying off. Always a chore, since it meant standing and waiting; otherwise, he'd wipe most of the oil off with a towel.

He did pat his hand dry before flicking the switch for the fan, spreading his arms wide.

"You're looking pretty good, cousin."

Lina stood in the doorway.

He swore, spinning away from her. "Really?"

"Your butt too. Nice."

"Lina, do you have a reason to be here?"

"Of course. I'm harvesting someone in the building – scraggly fellow, died on the toilet."

"Fine." He raised a hand. "And just in case, don't tell me it's a more common place to die than you think, because I know that already."

"You're especially grumpy today, Reed."

A new voice chuckled. "Reed? What are you doing?"

"Preparing to head to the Fringe. Obviously."

"Ah. You know those particular methods of yours are only fifty percent effective."

"This isn't my only precaution."

"I know; I'm just stirring you."

"God, Max – do you both really have to watch me while I dry off?"

"I suppose it's optional... but we're not here to judge you or ogle you, if that's what you're worried about."

"I might be," Lina added.

"*What do you want?*"

"Just to give you an update and see if you need anything before you head off after Valen."

"I was hoping you'd both be along for at least part of the trip – I assume Potter won't be coming?"

"No, he's still looking a little... thin," Lina said and it sounded like she smirked as she spoke.

"We might be able to come along for some of the way," Max said.

"Good."

"So, what's your plan?" Lina asked.

"I'm going to ask Lily to see if there's anything floating around out there about Emerald and deliver a message to her brother at the same time."

"That ghost you used before?"

"Hence the Fringe."

"Think she'll hear you better from the Fringe?" Max asked.

"I'm hoping so – otherwise I'm out of ideas, short of blindly charging off to the east."

"You're still breaking the rules, aren't you?" Lina asked.

"Not if she just 'happens across me' somehow."

"How?"

"I have an idea for that... but it'll have to wait. If you really want to help, why don't you search a house for me. And an office – Alan Dunstall."

"What are we looking for?" Lina asked.

"Anything linking him to Garibaldi or Elise Roberts' murder." Reed sighed. "And if you could do it right now, that'd be fantastic."

"Sure thing."

Silence followed and Reed glanced over his shoulder to make sure the two were gone before reaching for a silver barrel-band ring that rested on his basin; clear image of the Glass Butterfly within. Using the ring would, like the Mexican insect it was named after, afford him a certain amount of camouflage, fooling eyes – living and spectral – into believing he was simply part of the landscape.

Next, he dressed in his usual jeans and dark jacket, his clothing snagging a little on his oily skin, and collected the Sonorous and his car keys, and phone... and gun, though it was probably only a precaution, since none of it would be heading beyond the Fringe with him anyway. *And they're too bloody expensive to have them fry down into a puddle.*

After locking up, Reed dashed along the hall, racing the elevator's moving light, and when the doors beeped open, he joined an older couple within. They were dressed quite smartly and they spoke together softly on the way down to the lobby. As the two exited, they clasped hands and a little twinge of fear caught in his chest; how long until one of his cousins or Aunty herself came to take one of them away?

For now, he had a job to do.

***

Reed glanced away and quickened his step as he passed the childrens' graves and their hopelessly bright balloons, heading deeper into the central part of the cemetery. Avoiding that particular section altogether was his original intention but he'd been forced further along the smooth roads by mourners, two separate funerals finishing in different parts.

Yet finally, he found a quiet spot, half-concealed by trees and the darkening afternoon, clouds rumbling across the sky. "Fitting."

No sophisticated ritual was needed to reach the Fringe in a cemetery – all he had to do was open himself to the other realm, let that side of his heritage recognise what was always all around... and there it was: an ash-like haze, the trees blackened and brittle, the stone headstones crumbling.

And most telling, the odd heat that came with the Fringe – as though the living part of him was suddenly working overtime to hold on. And maybe it was? He'd never asked. But at least his precautions were taking the edge off the oppressive atmosphere.

He strode along the Fringe, keeping his distance when it came to the darker spots where the Underworld drew closer. Few spirits were about – nearby, a girl in a white gown sat perched on her headstone, her chin lifted as though she sang. Her voice was soundless and she did not notice him.

Either lost in her memories... or his wards were enough.

But Lily's headstone stood not so far away; he twisted between a middle-aged couple who stood smoking together in suit and evening gown, and stopped before Lily's grave. The weathered stone was impossible to read from the Fringe, nevertheless, he knew it was hers.

Reed bent down and raised a hand to knock on the stone – and the sound that followed was not unlike someone rapping on a front door.

Lily appeared in her green and yellow floral dress, a frown on her face – but it faded when she recognised him. "Reed! I didn't think we could speak again."

"It's more that I cannot *call* you specifically," he said. "But in the Fringe, it's a little different – I can find you. Normal people can't do this."

"You're going to get in trouble anyway, aren't you?"

He shrugged. "It's worth it; I need your help."

"Again?" She folded her arms. "Aren't *you* supposed to be helping *me* now?"

"If you could find a man for me and–"

"Only if you do something extra for me."

"Yes?"

"It's kinda big."

"I'll do my best."

"Well, I want you to make sure that when it is my time, that my Next Swim is a musical one."

He blinked. A soul's repurposing was something only Aunty could arrange, a request she might even grant him actually, but the request itself was a surprise. Ghosts usually wanted more lavish things. "I think I can do that."

"Good." Then she frowned. "Are you judging me or what?"

"No. It's just that no-one has ever asked me something like that."

"Well I'm asking – okay?"

"It certainly is."

"All right then. So, who am I searching for?"

Reed outlined what he wanted in regard to Valen and sent her off with a stern warning. It was unlikely that the cultists would attempt to 'Vanish' her or that they'd even notice a young ghost... but he owed her a warning at a bare minimum, after all, *she* was taking the risk.

He leant against the back of her headstone to wait. It wouldn't be a long one – ghosts tended to be pretty damn fast.

Something shimmered within a nearby shadow.

Reed grew still.

A willowy figure stepped forth, long white hair floating around the shape as though it slid through water. A White Hunter. *Shit.* He froze – the thing was serious trouble if it decided to be. Vaguely feminine beneath the pale robe, its face was blank save for a bright red mouth that glistened with blood. Drops of red fell to evaporate in the air as it swung its sightless head across the cemetery – slowing when it faced him.

"Damn."

The Hunter spun closer, eating up the space between them and looming over Reed. Up close, the face was larger than human and the blood continued to drip from its mouth – yet did not strike Reed. He held his breath – reaching slowly for Sonorous. It might not be enough, but the bell was a last resort because between the Glass Butterfly and Aunty's Ward he'd be fine... surely.

Please.

Reed stared back at the Underworld creature.

Its head swayed now, not unlike a cobra.

Sharp, pointed teeth were just as red as the rest of the mouth, along with a forked tongue that darted out as if to test the air – which it was – the Hunter wanted to taste him first.

A hiss followed.

Still he held the bell. If it turned out the Sonorous wasn't enough, the chime would only enrage the Hunter. Better to remain hidden; the mark of Mors was enough surely, it had been in the past and nothing had changed now... had it?

The handle dug into his fingers as he clenched.

White hair spread forth and it snaked out to brush his cheek – and then the Hunter straightened. It spun and started across the cemetery, almost flouncing... and he raised his hand to his cheek; numbness spreading.

Safe.

Reed exhaled, slumping back into the stone.

Chapter 19.

"I think they've moved." Lily's voice echoed from her headstone.

He stood beside her grave, resting one hand upon the cool stone, heart still beating a little quicker than usual. It had taken her a moment to 'find' him, now that he'd left the Fringe.

His cheek was still numb too but at least he'd escaped unscathed. And while he'd not come close to his limit for staying within the Fringe, the brush with the White Hunter had certainly been enough to instil some additional caution within him.

Reed sighed. "So they were at Emerald at one time?"

"I think so; it felt strange. Like a lot of people had been there, and something... bigger than me, not alive. Not dead either, I don't really understand."

No doubt the Goddess. "Was there a trail leading away from the lake?"

"Yeah, more than one – but I think most of them came here, to the city."

He straightened. "Where?"

"The Botanical Gardens."

"That sort of makes sense."

"They were easy to find once I knew their smell, and Valen too. But he's trapped, like in a tower, I think." She paused. "It was all a little too strange, Reed. It felt wrong."

"I'm sorry, Lily. But you did a great job and I'll make sure Aunty grants your request – you have my word."

"I'd better."

"You can trust me," he replied. "She'll owe me once I rescue Valen."

The sense of her smile came through her spectral voice. "Good."

And then she was gone.

Reed lifted his hand and stared up to the sky, which had cleared a little, and no longer suggested the threat of rain, but it hadn't grown any warmer. He pulled his coat closer as he started across the cold lawns back toward the car park.

If he was lucky, he'd have time to collect a few things then get to the Gardens before they closed up for the night.

Either way, he had the cult's location at last.

Get ready, you bastards.

***

Even if Emerald had been a false trail or perhaps a temporary base of operations for the cult, the importance of water turned out to be true enough; since the Shining Leaves now lay within the Royal Botanic Gardens with its artificial lake.

And it did make sense, considering who their master was... but what had shielded them from being sensed? How long since they actually left Emerald?

He had no answers.

In the gardens, crowds were thinning out as dusk swept down on the city. First the tops of the skyscrapers and then the orange light spilt over to fill the Ornamental Lake and tint the leaves, the benches and various sheds, pavilions and toilet blocks, seeming to even dull the voices of children as they exited, weary-seeming parents in tow – though all were smiling.

And why not? It was a beautiful, if manicured place, and without knowing that Feronia's minions were plotting... something terrible within its walls, why wouldn't you enjoy it?

"Not so for me," Reed breathed. He shifted where he sat on the cold earth within his vantage point, concealed inside the shrubbery. It still wasn't clear what he was looking for – a literal door to their hiding place? Did it span the Fringe? At least *something* about the Shining Leaves' lair had to be accessible to regular people, or else humans wouldn't be involved.

For what had to be the twentieth time, he checked the bag he'd put together.

Gun, knife, bat, Sonorous and... a litre of Roundup. Reed almost laughed. But he had also painted a pair of solar crosses or 'Chariot Wheels' on the backs of his hands. A little help from Sol's fiery chariot – another last resort.

And it wasn't enough.

The fierceness that had him striding from the cemetery earlier had waned. But what other choice did he have? No-

one could help him, not with what he was about to face...
only his cousins. Yet they'd been forbidden by Aunty. She
didn't want to risk *them* but that concern obviously didn't
fully extend to him, it seemed. He did have an advantage,
being able to stay present in the living side of the Fringe
as long as he liked, but more than that – Lily had provided
him with something useful when it came to Valen, not
only was he 'alive' but he was in a tower.

Still, even that wasn't a lot.

When it finally grew dark enough to begin his search
he rose with a groan; his legs were stiff – pins and needles
leapt forth in an assault. Yet he didn't have long to complain
to himself about it. A flickering green light appeared on
one of the islands, like a slice within the very air. Nothing
a normal human would see; the suggestion of the Fringe
was clear in the way grey fought between glimpses of green.

Did Aunty truly expect him to go in there alone?

No.

"This is pure fucking madness." He crouched at the
edge of the water and dropped a coin within. "With this
token I call upon Mors. Let her hear my mortal voice; a
whisper across water."

Ripples in the surface stilled far too swiftly and a skull
appeared – and she was frowning. "I am quite busy, Reed."

"Don't dismiss me, Aunty – this is serious."

"Everything is serious."

"I'm glad we agree," he said. "I'm talking about Treveyos
– I can hardly go in there alone to face him and his lackeys.
I don't even know how many of *what* will be waiting."

"Hmmm."

He waited.

"You are more capable than you believe."

"Even if that's true I'm still just one, Aunty."

The skull's eyes narrowed. "Are you somehow trying to avoid your duties?"

He sighed, hanging his head a moment. *This isn't working.* A different approach, perhaps. "Look at it this way. If I'm right and I'm no match for what's in there, then you lose a valuable tool, right? I'm the only family member who can live on this side of the Fringe. Do you really want to risk me?"

"You are not the only one, actually."

He blinked.

"Yet your argument is sound. I will send someone."

And then she was gone.

Reed sat back. Not the only one? *Who else is out there? Do I have brother or a sister? A living cousin? What the hell, Aunty.* No-one had ever mentioned another mostly human family member... he ran a hand through his hair. That was a problem for later. Now, he had to know, just who was she sending?

"Let's get going, Reed."

He spun.

Adrina stood behind him, arms folded. As before, her hair was arranged in a wreath and she wore a simple brown tunic and bare feet – though her tall longbow was not present. Yet the same bright blue eyes stared across at the green hole in the world.

Based on Adrina's attitude with the Scale Fiend, she'd either be all too happy to actually help or she'd have been sent to observe – in which case she'd have information at least.

"Ah... did Aunty fill you in?"

"I know what we're here for, yes. How are you planning on getting over there?"

"Wait, do you know what we're going up against?"

"I told you, yes."

"Then fill *me* in, will you?"

She sighed. "It's yet another trap, this time in their actual lair – yet nothing that could hold you because once again, this is aimed at your cousins specifically. My Lady tells me that Treveyos wants more of Death's children."

"Then we can spring it and save Valen – you aren't in equal danger?"

"Of course I am but I have a few advantages Max, Lina and the others lack, so trust me and get moving."

Reed raised an eyebrow. It wasn't all the information he'd have liked but it was actually more than he'd expected. "And the so-called Shining Leaves?"

"We'll find out how many, if any, are inside when we get there."

"In a tower?"

"Yes – it's beyond the Fringe, we'll have to find the right passage. How long can you survive in there?"

"I've never tested it but probably a day." And more, he still bore Aunty's mark, the oils and the Glass Butterfly ring.

She nodded. "That should be more than sufficient. I'll meet you there."

Her voice echoed in the darkness, as though her body had moved too quickly – which it probably had. She winked into view on the island as he ran along the bank, stopping at the small pier for the seemingly ungraceful, gondola-like boats.

"Here we go then."

The pair of bolt cutters he'd brought along for the ride freed one of the boats and then he was poling himself toward the island. It'd be an unpleasant surprise for tomorrow's tourists and the operators but at least nothing was going to be broken.

Any breaking was going to happen elsewhere.

Adrina stood tapping her fingers upon her arm when he arrived. Her longbow snapped into view and she strode through the rift without a word. He didn't bother calling for her to wait but hurried after.

The green slice was as air – he passed into the Fringe without feeling it and then the grey took over, the pressure and heat snapping down around him. No sign of any ghouls or Sneaks at least. He grimaced. Adrina stood nearby, bent over the ground. A thin thread of green led into the island's trees... and disappeared.

"All we have to do is follow it, right? If it's a trap, there shouldn't be many detours."

She nodded. "Most likely but I can feel the trail split."

"That's more than me."

"One leads to the true lair, perhaps. And one the trap."

"The trap first," he said. "That's where Valen will be."

She rose and drew an arrow from her quiver in the same fluid motion. "Agreed."

Adrina led him through the branches and into a tiny clearing where another slice in the very world waited, bearing the same green flecks, though it had been joined by yellow now rather than grey.

"Be ready." Adrina passed through.

Chapter 20.

He stepped into a forest smothered by green.

Even the light beneath the trees bore the same tint, as though the tumbling vines and wild moss gave off a glow that should have been artificial... but it was not. An organic taste lingered in the air. The place weighed upon him not unlike the Fringe, thick with scents of earth and plants, and something pungent... decay.

And for every green leaf there lurked a yellowing or brown counterpart, generally hidden beneath healthier plants. One vine had split open to spread dark green muck across a fallen trunk. When one of the leaves fluttered down it hit a ground damp with rot. Adrina's feet squelched as she started forward but she did not react.

Reed thanked his own foresight – the perfect day to choose boots over runners.

"This is Feronia's domain?"

Adrina nodded. "Though the rot is not something I expected from a goddess of Abundance. Something is very wrong here, Reed."

"Let's focus on Valen first."

"Very well." She pointed. "There."

Glimpses of dark stone between the trunks and drooping branches, most overladen with fruit turned purple or sometimes black. He stepped around puddles of mango and passionfruit, heaped with beetles and maggots, the stench of decay twisted with a sweetness that caught in his throat.

He fought off a gag.

Though Adrina scanned the trees with her eyes almost constantly, they encountered nothing but the ruin of fertility on their path to the grand, oaken door that barred entry to the tower. It was a squat thing covered in greying vines but a pink rose grew at the base, seemingly unharmed by the blight.

Diana's servant pushed on the door and it opened without creak or scrape.

Reed joined her, one hand on his bell and the other clutching the gun – a weapon for either possibility. Hopefully its brief exposure to the Fringe had not harmed it either... not that he relished the thought of personally slaying the cultists with his bullets.

And yet, it was a naive thought.

Someone or something had to die to make everything right, surely? *And it's not going to be me.*

Inside, light fell upon a black-robed figure tied to a stone pillar. The pillar had been decorated with carven flowers, most bearing delicate petals and ripe fruit, the bindings made of a purple vine. Unlike the other vines these were strong and healthy, even pulsing slightly, seemingly of their own accord.

Valen.

His head hung upon his chest, golden hair gleaming in the light, giving him an air of wellness, yet he was motionless – not Vanished or Emptied, that Reed would have sensed – but nor did he respond to his name.

Reed glared into the dimness of the tower; it was just an empty room. "They're taking their time."

"Check on Valen."

He crossed the room and reached up. The vines were tight, too strong to tear away so he drew his knife and sliced through one. Valen's arm swung free and Reed caught him, supporting his slight weight easily while he worked on the other vine.

"Done."

He lowered Valen to the cold floor, peering closely at his cousin as the man blinked his eyes open; they were a startling grey, somehow kind and old and patient and determined all at once – nothing had changed. He still bore the movie star good looks that were actually best described as deeply unfair, but the guy was so damn nice it was impossible to resent him for it.

"Valen, can you hear me?"

His eyes focused. "Reed. Thank you for coming." His voice was a whisper, though he smiled through tears. "I hate to worry you but I don't feel up to a daring escape, right now."

"I can send you back now." Reed lifted Sonorous.

His cousin lifted an eyebrow. "Not my favourite method of travel but I understand."

Adrina drew near. "What did they use you for, Valen?"

"Greetings, sweet Adrina," Valen replied. "Treveyos has used me to channel power for more than one purpose but it mostly goes toward the maintenance of a single flower. I think I know *why* but not the specifics of how they are able to use me in the first place – which is troubling."

"Then they'll be disappointed when they find me and Reed."

"I imagine so."

"All the more a reason to leave now," Adrina said.

"I must disagree – please stay a little longer, after all, you are honoured guests," a new, deep voice announced. Treveyos stood at the mouth of the tower, arms folded across his giant chest.

"Shit." Reed rang Sonorous.

Valen winced but faded quickly, unable to resist the call in such a weakened state. Only stone and scraps of vine remained behind and Reed stood, drawing his gun. Adrina stepped closer, her bow raised as half a dozen of the robed cult members filed into the room, all armed with their customary Fasces.

While Adrina was forbidden to kill humans, there was nothing to say she couldn't hurt them – and her arrows were swifter than any bullet.

But Reed hesitated to offer any sort of attack.

Treveyos had made no aggressive gestures; he did not even appear concerned at the loss of Valen... something was wrong. "The trap is something else," Reed told Adrina.

"Very much so." The big man smiled. "But we have what we sought now."

"And what do you mean by that, human?" Diana's servant asked.

Reed sucked in a breath. Treveyos had known all along that Aunty would be reluctant to send any more of her children... *Was he betting on* me *being sent instead of Max or Lina?* But why? As a tool? It made little sense; Reed's power was generally innate to him – it was nothing other humans could use. No, most of his power rested in his ability to Take Time or use artefacts that...

He froze.

Use artefacts?

"That's it. Shit, take this." Reed shoved Sonorous at Adrina. "Hurry."

"Capture them!" Treveyos roared.

The Shining Leaves swarmed forth.

"Don't be foolish," Adrina snapped.

"They want the bell."

"What?"

"They can't have this," he shouted, and pushed Sonorous against her and now she took it, a frown on her face. "Go," he cried.

Reed lifted his gun and the nearest man hesitated. "That's enough."

The cultist's jaw clenched – most of his gaze now focused on Adrina.

"You'd better have a plan," Adrina said, then she was gone.

Curses rang out.

Reed backed across the stone floor, weapon weaving between cultists, holding them at bay as he glanced around. No holes in the wall, no windows, not even stairs. Trapped.

"Surrender," Treveyos called. "Or, kill us all and ruin your life."

"No-one will find your bodies," Reed replied. Was it even true? Impossible to know one way or another. Yet when he'd killed before it tended to be during life or death struggles and once, an accident during his youth... but murdering seven people now, could he even manage it? Even if the cultists were damn villains?

"Mr Lavender, you don't even know where *you* are," Treveyos said with a chuckle. "And believe me, I have taken all the necessary precautions to ensure that you will not only be caught but that the Shining Leaves will live on. So, will you not surrender?"

The bastard was right.

And if he was bluffing... well, he was doing a good job.

The big man folded his arms, beard bristling. "If you give up peacefully, I will even tell you the truth about your parents."

Reed lowered his gun.

Chapter 21.

"What?"

No-one knew how to find his parents.

Reed had searched. Begged, *pleaded* with his grandfather. With Aunty herself – dozens of times, and even once with Potter.

Yet his tears had been as nothing.

Nothing against viciously iron-clad laws that had remained sacrosanct for eons. Longer. And even if for good reason, it hadn't felt that way all those years ago.

"Surely you haven't forgotten?"

"I remember," Reed spat. "But that's nothing you can offer."

"It was just before your birthday was it not? Summer holidays, you had been out riding your bike with friends. When you returned home, only an empty house – but I can tell you what the symbols covering the kitchen meant." The man strode forward now. "Cooperate and you will see. I admit, I did want your Sonorous quite keenly but even without the bell you could still do great good for the lands."

"You're full of shit."

"Am I? Either way, you have to decide. Attempt to shoot each and every one of us or surrender."

Reed lifted the gun, jaw clenched. The barrel shook and he gripped harder, tensing his muscles. The trigger was like a lead weight; even a feather touch was somehow unimaginable. *I can't just slaughter them, god damn it!*

Treveyos was smiling.

He knew, the bastard.

"Fine." Reed tossed the gun to the stones. It clattered to one of the cultists. The rest surged forward now, relieving him of his bag and gripping him by the upper arms.

"My story certainly sparked your interest," Treveyos said.

"I don't believe you at all – I'm just not a fucking murderer."

Treveyos shrugged and turned to leave. "Either way I am pleased. Let me show you what you cannot see, give you a chance to earn your keep, now that we'll be feeding you."

Someone shoved Reed.

He stumbled out of the tower behind the cult leader, following the man through the scent of rotting vegetation. The path meandered but it ran essentially to the left of the main trail leading back to the Fringe, but he noted it only absently – was Treveyos telling the truth? Or was it a bluff?

The bastard knows a lot about that day.

And the symbols.

Not even the police had seen those. Reed had scrubbed each one clean but even now, they were as bright as day in his mind. Right down to the *scent* of whatever had been used to make them, like hot sand or ancient stone... and the shape, silvery scrawls... but there had been order.

A pair of opposite-facing half-circles seemed important

among the symbols on the dishwasher, the kitchen cupboards with their 'rail fence spirals' or the floor, where so much had been written but so little made sense – and yet, no hard angles to any of it, no squared edges to the symbols, everything flowing.

Treveyos stopped.

Reed blinked. They'd reached a clearing ringed by evenly spaced thistles, tall as streetlights. Beyond that in turn, a ring of Shining Leaves two deep, some facing outward and some facing the shape within.

"Behold her infancy," Treveyos said.

'Her' referred to figure reclining upon a throne of moss, a vaguely-humanoid shape of vines and leaves, slug-like limbs slung across one arm, tiny flowers of blue blooming and withering in a hypnotic cycle as it pulsed; the approximation of a faceless head swivelling to regard him.

Reed shivered.

Even unfinished, even without eyes or mouth, the sense of a vast, all-encompassing presence bore down upon him. More, it sought him, a force upon his very shoulders. His knees strained but did not buckle – and then the force eased.

Was it testing me?

"Then this is Feronia?" Reed asked. Had she been at full strength, no doubt her test – if that's what it had been – would have been far more troubling.

"In time, yes." Treveyos cast a loving, almost proud gaze across the figure on the throne.

"And your purpose?"

"Should be obvious to you."

Reed clenched his jaw. "Enlighten me."

"Reclamation, obviously." Treveyos raised an eyebrow. "Humanity has encroached upon the natural world too deeply and for far too long now. It is time to take control of the earth once more, to return this world to a state Feronia envisions. For her – for *our* survival."

"Humanity is part of the earth."

"A poisonous part, surely you can see that?"

"Fine, Treveyos. So, you restore Feronia and she sends her flora and fauna rampaging across the cities and what? Wipes out humanity – where does that leave you and your precious Shining Leaves?"

He smiled. "As a rare species indeed, preserved and protected."

"That's a zoo."

"Sacrifices must be made for the greater good – come now, where is your utilitarian spirit?"

"I don't see Bentham or Singer agreeing with you." Reed glanced over at the as yet unfinished restoration of the Goddess. How were they actually bringing her forth? The circle of cult members seemed to be breathing hard – or at least deeply, something he hadn't noticed at first. Even as he watched, a robed man fell to one knee with a grunt.

He was replaced by a robed woman who approached from another path, and who took up his Fasces without a word.

The man who had fallen pulled himself from the circle and crawled off in the direction his replacement had come.

"Curious?" Treveyos asked. "Well, if you will accompany me back to the tower, you can discover exactly how we are drawing the necessary energy from beyond the Fringe – you will, in fact, be instrumental in continuing the process until a replacement comes for you."

"No-one is falling for your trap again."

"I am confident that there will be at least one more fool among you," he replied, raising a hand to gesture away from the clearing, as if merely accompanying an honoured guest from one place to another. "I'll let you lead the way."

Reed preceded the man back along the path to the tower, where a pair of the robed fools pushed him against the stone column and lifted a set of vines, which they used to pin him to the stone. And while the cultists left his forearms and legs free, the vines tightened against his chest by themselves, impairing but not stopping his breathing.

Next, the Shining Leaves affixed a ring of Fasces into the floor before him and left.

"Please stick around while we continue our ritual – the Fasces will look after you," Treveyos said with a grin, though his eyes did not reflect a shred of warmth.

Reed ignored the supremely sophisticated attempt at humour. It seemed that Treveyos *did* feel the loss of Valen after all. Good, a small mercy.

Next came freedom.

However he was going to manage that...

Being tied to the column was one thing; another was the growing closeness of the Fringe, which flickered at the edges of his vision. It was not completely present, nor had he himself slipped within, but it seemed the circle before him was helping to bring the Fringe forth – the tools were reacting to him, to his Death-side, like a humming against his skin.

It also kept a hold on the Fringe, enabling it to linger perhaps – though not so consistently as using Valen must have enabled. "Not as good using a half-skull, I guess," Reed muttered.

Whatever amount of energy was being channelled from the Underworld and through the Fringe to the bundle of vines on her moss throne seemed at least *somewhat* dependant on his presence and so escape would obviously serve more than one goal.

Reed twisted his torso as best he could – and the vines constricted. He gasped. After a moment, the vines loosened again, still firm. He lifted his forearm as best he could – just testing – and once more, the vines squeezed.

"Fine."

He lowered his arm.

Shit, there has to be a way.

The Shining Leaves took everything he'd bought into their lair. He was trapped and his family couldn't save him – that left Adrina but she hadn't reappeared yet and who knew when she'd be back... or even whether? "It's up to me."

He lifted his hands – and there, the twin Solar Crosses.

Reed exhaled, a spark of hope flickering.

Burn the vines.

Treveyos hadn't recognised them, nor any of his servants. It was a true blessing, but they were hardly well-known symbols, since so few were ever allowed to learn them.

Still, the cost was great; Sol would expect something in return. And who knew what the god would ask, or whether Reed would even survive delivering upon any such request. The symbols had always meant to be a last, desperate resort.

Isn't that this very moment?

Things *were* quite grim.

On the other hand, Treveyos would definitely keep him

alive to feed Feronia, at least until someone else turned up. In a way, the threat wasn't immediate – at least, not to his life. He sighed. But feeding the Goddess was not something he could be responsible for since she wasn't precisely in her right mind – if such a thing could be said of the gods at all.

Reed lifted his forearms as he looked down. He just had to get the chariots to touch, that was all, then he'd be free. "Come on." His limbs began to tremble as he strained against his bones. The vines responded by tightening, restricting further movement.

"No."

He pushed harder, fingers crossing. Just a little more and –

Something cracked.

Reed screamed. Pain erupted in his side, spreading around his rib. A cracked bone? He blinked through a haze of pain. Somehow, he'd kept his hands close together. He turned one wrist and the backs of his palms met.

Fire exploded around him.

The vines were gone in a flash. He pitched forward, growling at fresh pain in his rib. But he stumbled forward despite it, falling to one knee and breathing hard – each draw a lance of agony. He let the borrowed flame die away and took another few desperate steps, approaching the nearest Fasces.

Tears streamed down his cheeks but he had to keep moving, had to escape. Who knew how much time he had?

Shouts rose from beyond the tower.

"Bastards," Reed gasped. A mistake. More pain swelled. He couldn't escape the tower, couldn't reach the exit to the Botanical Gardens, let alone outrun anyone if he tried. Couldn't fight. Couldn't hide. They'd catch him so damn easily. Which left only one option, another stupid risk. "The Fringe.

Though it would probably kill him, Treveyos and his cronies couldn't follow.

No other choice.

"Fucking hell."

Reed slowed to clutch at his side. *Do it, fool.* He squinted at the flickers of grey, opening himself up to the beyond.

The tower walls vanished.

In their place, crumbled piles of grey stone that exposed him to world devoid of colour, just a hush that waited, as though moments before a terrible storm. Clouds twisted like grave worms above and the landscape was desolate, no green plants or trees here, mostly withered roots, stumps and mud to go with the scent of stagnant water.

And approaching figures.

Ghouls, hopping across the blackened earth with their stunted blue bodies and glowing eyes, Sneaks flitting from grey stump to stump and beyond them two taller shapes; White Hunters, their flowing hair and spindly bodies nearing at a more leisurely pace.

Reed fell back several steps, wincing as he did.

His skin began to tingle from the atmosphere. There was a sharpness to the feeling now, as if it was getting ready to flake away. Which meant his preventative measures were faltering. *Like the ribs and now two bloody White Hunters aren't enough.*

He glanced at the back of one hand, the Solar Cross had burned away, and the other would be the same. He was out of options and most definitely alone. His heart thumped an odd, double pump. *Like it heard me.* His pulse thundered through his veins and even that seemed to cause stabbing pain in his chest, but he did his best to keep his breathing shallow.

The Ghouls arrived. They flowed over the stumps of stone, beady eyes bright as they surrounded him and paused. One reached out a clawed hand.

"Back!" Reed hissed.

It withdrew with a gurgle but did not leave.

His Word was not powerful enough for that – being only half-related to Death. Reed lifted his voice. "Aunty!"

But there was no answer, just more agony.

The White Hunters had drawn close enough for the red of their mouths to become visible.

Think, idiot, think!

A formal call was impossible without water. There was no guarantee she'd hear him if he continued to call but it wasn't unheard of, especially from within the Fringe. The more chilling thought was that she would hear and not bother.

After all, Valen was free and she'd told him herself – he wasn't the only 'half-skull' out there. She had replacement options if she needed another human to do her bidding.

Something crashed into the back of his knees.

He hit the stone with another scream, ribs burning.

A dark figure in twisting rags skipped over him, giggles left in its wake. *Damn Sneaks.*

Blue bodies closed in with eager chattering, sharp, guttural sounds that were not words but a language nonetheless, pressing against him, preventing escape – but they did not attack, instead their voices softened.

Reed's vision dimmed, the pain was taking over.

White loomed.

Drops of red swam down to strike his face but each drop was only a suggestion as numbness spread.

This is it, this is how I die.

Disappointment surged – he'd never learn the truth about his parents, never atone for any of his mistakes, never apologise properly to Emma for the way things ended...

Light flashed.

Blood filled the air like perfect, glistening beads. They floated up and away, moving so slowly. The hovering blue receded and something white bounced across the stone beside him but he was already fading away in shadow, into the Underworld.

Yet one more shape lingered, almost an after image – a scythe.

Chapter 22.

He woke to sunlight.

I'm floating.

Blue sky surrounded him, nothing below but white clouds and from somewhere, a soft breeze to tug at his clothing. No pain, no blood, no Underworld either – instead, a bright figure resolved before him, elongated limbs, but definitely human-like. Incandescent, warm, yet not blinding – Sol was controlling himself.

"You must thank your cousin, Mr Lavender."

The scythe? Potter! Reed almost groaned. *He'll love having one up on me again.* But the relief of being alive and not Dead or Vanished, well, that was worth any gloating Potter cared to do, which was, in all honesty, doubtful. *Noble git.*

"I will, Sol."

"Now onto business most swiftly: you used the Chariot Wheels. I trust you have not forgotten the conditions upon which I allow Demi-Gods and those such as yourself to borrow such fractions of my power?"

"I am in your debt."

"Yes, however, not mine precisely."

The bright figure changed and now, rather than being an all-encompassing glow, Sol's light became more specific, as though the sun flashed upon armour.

Sol Invictus.

A deeper but similar voice answered. "Precisely, Reed – so, are you ready to hear what I require from you?"

Reed nodded, though he was not prepared at all. How could he be? The soldier's deity could well ask for absolutely *anything* and refusal was impossible. More, if Reed was to believe Aunty, apparently even *failure* was not an acceptable outcome for those who accepted the task but couldn't live up to their side of the bargain.

But the moment he invoked the Solar Crosses he'd been bound.

About all he could ask was for a reasonable timeframe and even that was only if he was lucky, negotiating with Gods was... tricky.

"I doubt you are as ready as you think," Sol Invictus replied.

"But I have no choice."

Booming laughter. "Correct, but do not look so crestfallen. Mortals have always participated in our games, Reed. It is simply the way of things."

"Participated?"

"You have a better word for such assistance?"

"How about 'died for' your games, since that's usually what it amounts to."

"Then you'd better keep your wits about you for this one."

Reed tried to grin. "That's always my plan."

Sol Invictus seemed to be smiling. "Welcome news

indeed. Very well, whenever you feel recovered I'd like for you to locate one of my soldiers, Livius. He died back around Nero's reign down there. And when you find Livius, please do resurrect him."

Reed opened his mouth but Sol Invictus flared before he spoke. "I know you are going to say that only your Aunty can do such a thing, which means that I am obviously asking you to convince her."

"Which you cannot do yourself?" And the more important question perhaps, was why?

"Remember, Reed Lavender – while you do not have to begin immediately, I do expect results."

"But..." Reed trailed off as darkness replaced the boundless sky and its blazing deity.

He groaned. Had he just gotten off lightly, or was something else afoot, something that he was now mired within? Not that convincing Aunty would be easy in any event.

Exactly what I need, more intrigue.

But for now it had to be put aside. First, figure out exactly where he was and –

"Reed?"

A white room lit by warm lamps bloomed around him, cocooned by a thin curtain – the scent of 'beyond clean' like an assault... hospital. The scent was, at least, a tiny distraction from the pain in his ribs, which had returned with some glee, it seemed.

Detective Duong sat beside him, expression one of concern. "You alive or what?"

He winced as he straightened. "I think it's the 'or what' option to be honest."

"Supposedly you've got a cracked rib and bruising and you split your scalp too but you should survive."

"Good."

Duong leant back in the chair, tapping a finger on the armrest. "It took me a long time to find you, you know. What the hell were you doing in the Botanical Gardens? This have to do with your family emergency?"

"No. I was following a lead but it led to..." Reed trailed off. Family... had Treveyos been telling the truth?

"To what?" Duong asked.

But still Reed didn't continue – a figure passed through the curtain – Max in his shades. Max plopped himself on the end of the bed and drew a pack of Longbeach Menthols. Not exactly the classiest cigarette out there, but just as poisonous as the rest. He tapped one free and lit it. "Not that bad."

"Some thug," Reed finally answered Duong. "Could have been hired muscle working for Dunstall, I don't know. I think I'm pretty lucky at least."

Max nodded. "That'll probably stick." He blew some smoke over at Duong.

Duong stood with a sigh. "Shit, I could use a cigarette."

Reed hid a smile within a yawn, and he wasn't faking for the most part. Even though he'd just regained consciousness, weariness pressed down upon his limbs. His head surely weighed twice than usual and his ribs still seemed to be prodding him over and over, a muted sensation only masked by whatever painkillers dulled his system. "Have you found anything?"

"On that prick Dunstall? Just more obstruction from his lawyers but we're building a case, rounding up informants and low-level dealers for now."

"And Elise?"

"Nothing. I'm sorry, Reed."

"Once I'm back on my feet I'll keep looking," he said with another yawn.

Duong offered a tired-looking smile. "Don't rush it, all right? Come down and give me whatever you can on the bruiser when you're ready."

"I will."

Duong left and Max stood, taking the now-vacant seat. "My update will be a lot more interesting," he said.

"Is this a private room?" Reed asked. The moment Max finished with his news, Reed had an update of his own to share.

"Yes, so we can talk without anyone thinking you've lost your grip."

He stifled a yawn. "Then let me have it."

Max reached for a jug of water that stood on the wheeled table. "Here, drink this. I can find you some sugar or coffee if that'll keep you awake?"

"Still don't drink coffee." Reed downed the chilled water, which did make a bit of a difference – at least, it kinda hurt his teeth, if nothing else.

"Good, you're a cheap lunch date then. Firstly, you'll be pleased to know that Valen is recovering nicely. You'll be less pleased to hear that Potter was the one who saved you in the Fringe."

"Yeah, I guessed." But to hear that Valen was doing well was great news indeed. "What about Adrina?"

Max produced the Sonorous, placing it beside the water. "She's a stern one."

"Did you get a lecture?"

"Yes," Max said with a sigh. "She called Lina and I a 'pair of scatterbrained kids' which I felt was uncalled for."

"So she's that much older than you?"

He shrugged. "Only by a thousand or so years, not enough to be dishing out comments like that to be honest."

"Who likes to say that 'age is an attitude' and not a number?"

Max ran a hand through his dark hair. "Rhianne, wasn't it?"

"Did Lina find anything at Dunstall's place?"

"Yes. A white robe and a Fasces tucked away in a hidden room at his office."

Reed nodded slowly. "Maybe that shouldn't be a surprise, considering what his underling was up to in that house."

"There's more."

"Elise?"

"Lina seems to think that Elise had been in his office – along with another person you were interested in, Veronica Williams."

Reed straightened with a wince. "That bastard, what did he want with her?"

"We don't know. But only two things are likely, right? Either she was being lined up to deal or it was recruitment for the Shining Leaves; those people have to come from somewhere, right?"

"Hmmm." The far east of the state *did* have something of a reputation for having a few hippies and environmental activists... it was no Byron Bay, but was *that* the reason Elise had travelled to the city?

Better news, if true, for Irene, but whether the motive

had been drugs or something else, Elise was still gone. *And you still haven't solved her murder – you're not even close.*

"So what now, Cousin?" Max asked.

"I don't know. Dunstall is still overseas... I want to get to the bottom of Elise's murder but we might have to put a stop to Treveyos first. Did Valen tell you what's happening?"

Max flicked cigarette ash to the bed, though it dissolved before hitting the sheets. "Yes. Aunty is meeting with Diana and some of the others."

"I bet I can guess the outcome of that meeting," Reed said, shaking his head.

"Meaning?"

"What it always means – that we'll have to do all work, I suppose."

"Probably," he said with a grin. "But that's what keeps things from getting boring, you know."

"You sound like your sister."

"Fine, throw that in my face." Max stood, glancing at one of the walls – or, more likely, *through* one of the walls. "I have to go to work, sorry. But once you're more rested, I'm sure one of us will drop in with some news."

"Wait."

Max shimmered out of and then back into view. "What's wrong?"

"Treveyos tried to tell me he knew what happened to Mum and Dad."

"Shit."

"I know." Reed leant back into the pillow. "He knew things that I didn't tell the police – things only *we* know."

"Or whoever is responsible for their disappearance would know."

"That's what troubles me – does he really know, and does he have information from whoever was behind it all?"

"Well, it's possible he was able to... I don't know, somehow 'read' Valen's memories? It's not beyond someone like Feronia of course, but we both know old Big Beard is no God."

"So do I take it seriously?"

Max nodded slowly. "For now, why not? But first, let's deal with the mess our friend has made and then figure out what's true."

"Then you'll try and make sure he isn't killed before he speaks?"

"I will," Max said, his voice echoing as he vanished once more. "I'd better go and collect Mr Ronald; he's getting a little anxious."

"Thanks," Reed said, then slumped even further into the pillows, closing his eyes. *Good, maybe that will help with the pain.* And whatever Aunty's plan was, it had better be something more impressive than sending him back through the damn Fringe.

Chapter 23.

Recovery was slow.

The hospital sent him home the day after, but a week had passed now and he was at least able to sleep on his back instead of half-sitting up, and moving around during the day wasn't as painful. Still, lifting things or running was generally out of the question – not a great time to be out amongst it all.

Yet no-one from the family visited and Aunty did not answer his formal calls.

Did it mean she'd already made her decision or that she was still deliberating? Not being able to work on his problems properly had all too quickly become a problem on its own.

Only Duong checked in to take a report – Reed described the guy who'd attacked him at the golf course, a useful stand-in for the 'attack' in the Botanical Gardens and a convincing half-truth, then got back to work, which meant days spent forcing himself into proper posture at the computer.

But it did seem that the Shining Leaves had an online presence – only they labelled themselves as the Southern Environmental Defence Organisation. Publicly they were seeking "like-minded individuals to join us on a quest to expand national parks and increase nature's role in daily life". There was a mix of environmentalism, conservation slogans and 'nature retreat' offers mixed in with ads for shitty SEDO products.

Of course, the office of the Shining Leaves was located in the centre of the *city*.

And when Reed called them, their line about needing to be close to "existing power structures in order to influence policy" might have held water... if their true plans weren't actually about rendering society completely inoperable.

Still, it was one of two places he was going to visit – the other being the old tip he'd received from the thug; the Hi-Fi Bar. *Once I'm up to it, of course.* It was a place he should have checked long ago, if he was being honest. Even so, he'd made his choices. Juggling the concerns of the living and the dead rarely meant swift resolutions for either group.

Still, five more weeks for recovery was far too long; he'd have to get out there and take some more risks... even considering how badly the last one had gone. He sighed as he leant back, moving only slowly, desk chair creaking.

"Hey, you *did* save Valen," he murmured. And Treveyos's progress had been slowed now that the flow from Underworld to Fringe and then on to the land of the living had been reduced to whatever bare trickle the cultists could manage.

But what was the big fool up to?

Treveyos would have put some sort of contingency into

play surely... either that or he'd choose to bury his head for a while? Reed would have paced if possible. Even if the man *did* try and lay low, Aunty and the others would be looking for him.

Or already were.

Instead of pacing, Reed managed to make it to a post box to mail a letter to Matt Stephens. Faking its age with creases and some improvised postal stamps - a few 'RTS' notes had been one problem. He bypassed the handwriting issue by typing Lily's message verbatim but even reading it back to himself, her voice came through. How would the guy react when he received it? That's what concerned Reed – he never knew the best way to pass a message on. Maybe it would work better than the last time.

Back inside, rain pattered against the windows, a somewhat muted sound despite its strength. He paused in the kitchen to watch it slide down the glass for a time, gazing across to the other apartments, most with their blinds closed.

Yesterday's water sat in the smaller sink, a coin seeming to sulk at the bottom.

Was it worth calling again?

Or should he just pour a glass of milk, eat a few biscuits and write off the rest of the day? *After all, I'm not going to achieve much more from here, am I?*

The faint ringing of bells drifted into the room and Reed straightened; a little too quickly, considering the twinge of pain that followed. But the bells were a polite – and welcome – announcement of a pending visit, which had to mean...

"Reed?"

Valen stood in the lounge room, golden hair gleaming and his smile calming. He was, in effect, something like an angel of mercy to look at, even with the black robe and the scythe necklace of silver. The jewellery alone was something of an oddity, considering Valen's age – he was one of the 'young' ones after all. Not like Potter, the tedious traditionalist.

"Valen, thanks for calling first."

Reed's cousin crossed the room to hug him, his grip cold but welcome nevertheless. "I am relieved to see you up and about," the man said.

A grunt escaped Reed, but the pain was not important. "Same for you. Want to sit?"

"Of course – you're still in pain? Forgive me."

Reed waved a hand as he led Valen to the kitchen table. "It's fine; I'm healing. So, tell me, did Aunt Mors send you? Is something happening at last?"

"She did ask but I came of my own accord to thank you."

Reed smiled. *Nice to hear those words, especially considering Aunty wasn't rushing over to offer them.* "So, what about Treveyos?"

"We're going to cut him off from the Fringe."

"How?"

"Mother is going to close it – she's just had a hard time convincing the others, that's what's been taking so long."

Reed gaped.

"Take it easy, Cousin. She's only able to do it for a single night so we have to work quickly."

"We?"

"We're going to draw him out and then you are – in Mother's words – going to 'finish him off'," Valen said with a smile. "I think Max or Lina taught her that one."

Reed had to chuckle. "So, are we going after the cult or...?"

"No. I believe Treveyos will be lured into a place of Diana's choosing – she is most concerned about what is happening with Feronia. Once the cult members and their master have left their jungle-nest of decay, she will send someone to handle the so-called Resurrection, though 'Reawakening' is probably more accurate."

"Handle?"

Valen spread his hands. "They are confident, though they did not share their methods with one such as I."

As troubling as Feronia's possible return in the form of some twisted cornucopia was, Valen's news *did* suggest it was far beyond the scope of a mere 'half-skull'. And the fact that at least two of the Gods had essentially mobilised was troubling.

But it did mean that Treveyos could be *his* focus. *Which means another chance to ask about Mum and Dad.* "Should I make this official business, then?"

"Bringing in the police?"

"They could round up a lot of those Shining Leaves."

"Perhaps those left here in the city at least, but I believe that Diana also has a plan for them, leaving, once again, you to put a stop to Treveyos."

"Another euphemism?"

"How you manage it will be up to you, of course. I doubt Mother expects you to break too many rules of this place."

"I'd better get thinking, then. I have a few questions to ask him first."

Valen nodded, expression becoming somewhat crestfallen. "Maximus told me... I fear I may have been the vessel for his ill-gotten knowledge, though it is nothing I recall."

Reed put a hand on his cousin's shoulder. "We don't know how he found out, and even if it happened while you were captured, I don't blame you and I never will."

"That eases my mind, thank you." Valen smiled again, and it was a brilliant thing, so unlike the common notion of death as a spectre or skeletal figure. "I've also brought something to help – though I apologise for not sharing it immediately." He reached into an inner pocket of his robe and drew forth a thin vial of bright blue liquid; it moved like a richly coloured mercury, film-set or video-game beautiful. "This should fix up your rib."

"Is this..."

He nodded. "From Apollo – and no guilt about accepting it, since I didn't have to offer much at all in exchange."

"Really?"

"Yes, so drink up."

Reed took Apollo's medicine and held the liquid up to the window's light, and even on such a gloom-filled day, the colour was startlingly vivid. Reed lifted the vial to his lips and tilted his head: like swallowing snowmelt, pure and sharp, the medicine spread through his body so fast that it caused his limbs to jerk.

The vial fell but Valen caught it with a smile.

"Good stuff, I take it?"

Reed laughed. "Very." *Not a hint of a pain left in my ribs.* Even the headache he hadn't fully been aware of was gone. His shoulders and back bore no stiffness from the computer chair either, and even his eyes had widened, the spectre of sleep banished in a blue rush.

Yet the gift kept giving… a sense of true health followed, as though any possible toxicants had been banished, as though he was in sudden peak physical condition, muscles taut but flexible, somehow eager. *Like I should run a double marathon.*

He sighed but it was one of contentment.

Valen stood. "Do whatever else you will to prepare now, since Mother closes the Fringe at noon tomorrow."

"Where do you need me?"

"The Lake in Westgate Park," Valen replied.

"Ah, is that the one that turns pink from salt every summer?"

"Yes. Mother is using it to prevent Treveyos and any cultists he brings from planting Fasces."

"They can still be carried and held, right?"

"True. But we are reducing the overall number, which matters, believe me."

"I do," he said. "So, do I look for a barge or a rowboat or something?"

"Just the shores will be enough," Valen said, then gave a nod before disappearing.

Chapter 24.

Reed joined the line before the nightclub, warmed in no way by the glow from nearby fast food chains and all night convenience stores. The swoosh of cars and echoes of laughter rang out across the inner city street as he tapped his foot upon the gleaming footpath.

His breath steamed in the night air as he waited, thankful for his beanie. *Winter's really overstaying its welcome.*

When he reached the door he paid the cover charge with a grimace, though it was hardly an exorbitant price since up and coming thrash bands filled the bill rather than any of the Big Four or newer metal heroes. Still, until the police paid for his consulting services things were a little lean, and he'd got the invoice in quite promptly, thanks to his little injury.

Considering what he faced tomorrow, he had to take a chance to follow-up on the lead he'd overlooked too long – the thug's tip about the Old Royal. Maybe it was thin but he needed something. And if he found nothing tonight it'd be that much harder to make any real progress on Elise's case.

At least, on his own.

Moving with the crowd, he descended the narrow steps into the club, the bass and drums preceding any image of the band. Around him, folks who were going for Goth were mixed in with 'old-school' metal-heads wearing their jeans and faded black band tees, a sprinkling of surfer-looking dudes sifted in to the crowd too.

The demographics played out the same below, in the club, where he bypassed the moshpit and the thundering band, and went for the cyberpunk-coloured bar with all its silver, glass and blue and pink neons. He ordered a coke and turned in the chair.

It was exceptionally unlikely that the silver-haired man he was looking for would be strolling the floor, which meant some talk... or snooping had to start soon.

"You're the half-skull, aren't you?" a voice asked.

Reed turned back to the bar. One of the customers watched him, beer in hand. The man was pretty solidly built, not quite a gym-nut but he seemed to take care of himself. And based on the scent that was only partially masked by all the smoke machine fog and weed, the man was a werewolf.

"I am," Reed said.

"Right. I just wanted to let you know I was here, just to hear the band. Got nothing untoward planned tonight."

"Oh," Reed nodded slowly. "Thanks. I guess you've already been to see the local pack?"

"Told them I'm only passing through, yeah. Spoke to a big wolf, almost golden fur. Never seen anything like it."

"Devin."

"Right."

"And he mentioned me?"

"Not so much, it's more that I noticed your scent... it's a bit like bones, only I can't explain this but you Reapers tend to smell like *silence*." He raised his hands. "I know, it don't make much sense."

Reed nodded. "Yeah, I've heard that before."

"Well, nice to meet you," the fellow said, then headed toward the back of the crowd.

Reed scanned the rest of the room. A stair led up to a long balcony where a soft glow suggested another bar. Maybe there'd be a way in there? If he could find someone in charge maybe he could bullshit his way to a conversation with Mr Silver Hair. Posing as a booking agent for a band perhaps... he opened his wallet and thumbed through the business cards he kept on hand for just such an occasion.

There – Alex Greenwood, Agent and Manager.

A nice clean, black card with white text, complete with e-mail and mobile number. It looked good enough, in case he needed something more for the front. Maybe it was all a waste of time. If Silver Hair knew who Reed was by sight, then entering the venue was enough of a risk that an alias would make no difference one way or another.

Reed indicated to the barman that he was after another drink.

"Know if the owner's in tonight?" he asked.

"Could be," the barman said. "Mr Froud is usually here for part of the evening. If you want to speak to him, try Peter at the top of the stairs."

"Thanks."

Over on the stage, the band paused to explain the next song and voices from the crowd, mostly requests, rose above the tuneless background noodling of the clearly impatient guitarist. It also gave Reed a chance to ask the security at the top of the stairs whether Peter was around.

The big man jerked a thumb over his shoulder, to a small table set beside the second bar. Three men sat drinking, passing a paper or ledger between them. "Peter's the one with the beard."

"Thanks."

Reed approached the table and nodded in greeting, raising his voice to compete with the music. "Hi, I'm looking for Peter?"

"That's me." The bearded fellow closed the ledger and took a drink. His friends said nothing, though one started for the bar.

"My name is Alex Greenwood and I'm representing some local metal bands." He handed over the card.

"Haven't heard of you."

"I haven't been in Melbourne long. I only have two bands but I'd love to book one here. Are you the man to see about that? Or does Mr Froud make those decisions?"

"Nah, mate. I do all the work. He's just the boss," Peter said with a wink. His friend chuckled. "Why don't you send me a couple of links, I'll check your boys out."

"That'd be great," Reed said. But he needed more – access to Froud or even his office itself maybe, but the old "this isn't the toilet" act wasn't going to cut it if he was caught wandering around. He glanced over the balcony; he needed to say something. "These guys been around long?"

"Few years – you should check out the bassist," Peter said.

"Will do. Thanks again; I'll be in contact," Reed said, then headed for the balcony rail. There, he joined a few punters and stared down at the band, who were still playing pretty hard. And the bassist did seem good.

Reed let his eyes drift to the restless mass of the crowd.

What he needed was another ploy, since 'Alex' had only managed to open communications with the manager, not the owner. And it was entirely possible that Peter had no idea that his boss was a shady type.

Reed straightened.

A familiar face pushed through the edge of the crowd.

Well, hello again. Reed's would-be hitman from the golf course. Did that mean Froud was on the premises? Reed strode to the stairs and descended, keeping his target in sight. The thug was actually leaving, though even that might still be helpful. *If I can convince him to talk again, that is. So long as the poor guy doesn't have a heart attack.*

"Hold the door, buddy," he murmured as he followed.

Chapter 25.

Outside, the thug pulled his army-green coat close as he strode past the souvenir and fast food shops to turn down the first alley. Reed paused a moment before following, his pulse climbing a little – and it wasn't nerves so much as excitement. Was Apollo's wonder potion getting him riled up with all the energy it had bestowed?

Was it just the possibility of some answers?

Or are you just being stupid?

Froud had links to the Shining Leaves, no doubts there, but more likely, surely, this was a chance to learn more about Elise's murder. And she'd been waiting too long now for whatever measure of justice he could offer by solving her case.

When Reed reached the side street he dropped a coin, then paused to scoop it up, glancing after his target.

Not too far away, light spilled from someone's back door and beyond it in turn, a fancy sedan sat gleaming. The thug had approached the car and was now nodding as he spoke to whoever had rolled down a window. Froud, hopefully. Further on, puddles, trash and bins, along with solid thudding from the club, the sound drifting down from the access.

No-one else around.

Reed moved into the alley then leant against the bricks as if he was simply going to have a cigarette or look at his phone. The voices did not quite carry, but it was not long before the thug nodded and continued on his way.

The moment he was out of sight, Reed took a breath and dashed up behind the car.

He wrenched the back door open and burst inside.

Warm light illuminated a silver haired man in a fine suit, his nose bent as though it had once been broken. His eyes had widened and his face was red with outrage. "Who the fuck are you?"

Reed grinned. "Boo."

The man, presumably Froud himself, looked to his driver. "Mal, get this arsehole out of my car, will you?"

Mal, a balding man with a sneer, opened the driver's door.

"Hey. Slow down unless you want to chauffeur a dead man," Reed said. Keeping his arm out of sight, he extended his hand to point at Froud. Only it wasn't his hand precisely; it was the *bones* of his hand.

Froud's eyes widened, almost comically. "What the hell is this?"

"You can feel the grave, can't you?" Reed asked. "Let's hold hands a moment so we can talk. Mal, go have a cigarette."

The driver frowned. "Sir?"

"Do it," Froud said, lips tightening.

Mal got out, rocking the car slightly, and they were alone. Reed gripped Froud's hand and took a day, just ripped away as sharply as he could.

Froud's face paled with shock and confusion. "No!"

"Yes. And there's plenty more where that came from if you decide to lie."

"About what?" Froud almost squeaked the words. He was breathing hard, his limbs trembling where he sat.

"Why send your goon after me?"

He blinked. "That's you? You're supposed to be dead."

Reed laughed at the choice of words, not just the cliché but how it wasn't necessarily too far from some manner of truth. "Why?"

"Because you were getting too close with your investigation into that bloody girl."

"Good. Too close to...?"

"Some freak, fuck. I don't know his name," Froud said then added, quickly, "But the job came from my distributor. *He* knows this guy."

"Alan Dunstall, right?"

A nod.

"You're doing well, Mr Froud. Keep it up. Who actually killed Elise? Same guy you send after me?"

"Not Trent, someone else. I have his number."

"Let's write that down before I leave then. But first, I'll need some more information."

"About what?"

"*Why*, of course. Why kill the girl?"

Froud shook his head and now, despite frequent glances to Reed's hand, seemed a little calmer. "You'd have to ask Dunstall, that."

"I will, but I believe he's overseas right now."

"A shame," Froud said with a smirk.

Reed took more time – two days now, and Froud flinched so hard his head smacked into the window. The man groaned. "It *is* a shame, isn't it?" Reed said with a smile. "I guess I could haul your corpse into his office and see if that brings him home?"

"Wait!" Froud cried.

"Fine. Talk."

"It was probably cold feet, okay? She must have seen too much of the operation and wanted out. Alan doesn't let that shit happen."

"Well, he's really sealed his fate with that policy. Which leads me to my final question. How can I get to Dunstall?"

Froud ran his free hand through his hair, glancing down at the skeletal claw that gripped him as he squirmed. "I'm not that important to him."

"Meaning you don't know? Or that you're not effective leverage because he won't hesitate to have you killed if word gets out that you sang?"

"Shit, both!"

"You're probably right about at least half of that – but I'm pretty determined, Mr Froud. I'd like to leave with something other than that number you owe me, and if you can't give it to me I'll have to be far less gentle than I have been so far." Reed squeezed.

"All right! The casino. He spends a lot of time there but not to gamble. I've seen him myself."

"Keep talking."

"He's got a penthouse suite there. I saw him get in the elevator with cleaning staff more than once."

"What do you mean?"

"I mean, he never rides the elevator unless it's with cleaning staff. Won't get on with anyone else."

"Isn't that something?" Reed said. It didn't make any sense

at all but it was a lead – whether the man truly had a suite at the casino or not would be easy to verify too. "Let's have that number then."

Froud managed to write on one of Reed's fake business cards best he could and once Reed had the number, he clicked a finger gun at his prisoner. "Thanks for the help, old boy."

"What are you?" Froud asked, his eyes still wide.

"Think of me as an angry loner – only, one with lots of friends who are far scarier than me," Reed said with a grin. "And here's a warning disguised as an offer. If you have anyone you feel might be 'dead weight' in your organisation, maybe they're not committing enough crimes or something? Well, feel free to send them after me."

Chapter 26.

Reed strode the still-glistening streets in his long coat, black beanie pulled down over his ears. Probably not the most confidence-inspiring look, but the wind bore a bitter edge now that the rain had stopped. Once he'd left Froud and the bar it had poured the rest of the night and continued on and off as he'd prepared this morning too, leaving gutters everywhere overflowing, bearing withered leaves and cigarette butts on death rides into the storm water drains.

Somehow, his stunt with Froud had not only won him some potentially useful information to follow up on, but it had failed to burn off the energy he'd retained since taking Apollo's vial. Sleep had been fitful too – yet he still woke ready for whatever was to come; an almost ridiculous buoyancy to his step. *Shit, I actually feel younger.*

And maybe a little bit of it was take-away coffee? He'd slipped through the bustle of Flinders Street to grab one before reaching the location of the Southern Environmental Defence Organisation office, where lurked in a completely innocuous fashion. The ageing building bore its share of dull graffiti but the windows were quite clean – for the posters to stand out better, perhaps?

He paused at the door to glance at his watch – good, plenty of time to reach the Westgate Park Lake by noon.

And, hopefully, plenty of time for another lead to materialise. He still had no evidence anyone could use in a human court for Elise's murder. The number he'd received from Froud had been an unattended mailbox, but Reed left a message as a potential customer. Clumsy, but without having the police attempt to trace the number, it was about all he could do.

At least until *after* Treveyon had been dealt with.

Inside the refreshingly green office, resplendent with ferns, jade plants and flowers, Reed removed his beanie and smiled at the receptionist, a young woman sitting across from an older man at a desk, clicking away on his computer.

"Good morning, ah, my name's Evan and I'm interested in learning a bit more about what you guys do."

She tucked dark hair behind an ear and returned his smile "Oh, that's great. Were you thinking of donating or volunteering perhaps? We have a tree-planting event coming up next week, actually."

"Well, I was hoping to speak to someone, actually – I saw something about 'green living' on your website?"

She swivelled in her chair. "Absolutely. Maybe Jordan can help you with that?"

The man looked up, offering his own smile, though he squinted. He lifted a pair of glasses then waved Reed closer. "Yeah, I've got a moment – ah, can you join me in an office actually? That way we can give Tracy some peace."

"That'd be great," Reed said.

Jordan led the way to another office a little way down

the hall. He wore jeans and a jacket, business casual all the way. *Maybe he misses the comfort of the robes?* Reed missed half a step – the man's shoes... black with tan soles. *Runners*, not dress shoes. Like those he'd sensed at the golf course.

An unlikely coincidence?

The man opened the door and flicked on a light. No windows but a table with two chairs and a series of colourful pamphlets and brochures. "Take a seat, Evan – be with you in a minute, I'm just going to get a cup of tea. You good?" Jordan glanced at 'Evan's take-away coffee.

"Yep, thanks."

"Check out some of the info while you wait." He smiled as he left, his jaw becoming a little more square than Reed had first thought. In fact, the fellow seemed fairly trim too. Good posture... *A vaguely military look?* Reed shook his head; that was a stretch. Two or three details didn't add up to proof – and that went for the shoes too.

Still, if nothing else, sharing a room with the man would mean a chance to try and sense Echoes... though it had been quite some time since Elise's body had been moved to the golf course.

Reed leant back in the chair. But he had to check. Providing the man *was* actually involved, today wasn't the day to blunder in. Some more information on the organisation now and a search warrant later would probably do it. Maybe drop a few hints – pretend he was originally from the east, maybe Nowa Nowa, see if that got a reaction, then back off and return with Duong?

Or send Max or Lina in to snoop first?

There was always a chance bringing the police would be a waste of time – it was all pretty thin right now, but knowing what you were going to find *beforehand* was a great way to catch a liar if nothing else.

Reed glanced over at the doorway; Jordan was taking his time.

He'd barely finished the thought when footsteps approached. *Good, now we can find out –*

Treveyon walked through the door.

The big man was dressed in t-shirt and jeans, utterly unassuming and all the more sinister for it, so unlike the spectacle of his robed persona, and, disorienting enough to give him pause.

Reed finally shot to his feet but Treveyon was faster – he lunged forth and caught Reed by the throat.

"You."

Treveyon shoved him up against the wall, keeping his grip tight. Reed caught the man's wrist with his own hands, trying break free but Apollo's Elixir or no, he wasn't strong enough. Treveyon kept the pressure on, enough to cut off a shout but not to impede speech – not that anyone would come to his aid anyway.

"Wonderful to see you once more, Lavender," the man growled.

"An equal pleasure," Reed gasped out.

"Now, if you want to survive this day, tell me what your dear Aunty has been up to since you escaped."

"Laundry."

Treveyon slammed a fist into Reed's stomach. Reed gagged but kept his feet by virtue of still being pinned to the wall.

"How clever you are today. Try again." He squeezed.

Blood rushed to Reed's cheeks as he gasped for oxygen.

Treveyon eased up and Reed sucked in air, spluttering as he glared at the cult leader. "Something you won't like."

"Listen, worm. You have a final chance before I choke the life out of you and move on to someone else, since you are no longer any bloody use to me as bait."

"You'll kill me whether I speak or not."

"Maybe you're right," Treveyon said, and wrapped both hands around Reed's throat. He squeezed. Reed kicked out. His blows struck the man's side and stomach but Treveyon did not flinch; he kept squeezing.

Reed tore at the man's forearms and hands to no avail.

He's killing you!

There was no choice. Through dimming vision, Reed locked eyes with Treveyon.

Faster!

He sank into the pupils, ignoring a snarl, and there, the man's lifespan waited, ready to be manipulated at Reed's will. The span was long, but the white was littered with blotches of purple blight. Feronia's influence? A fleeting thought. Reed reached out and plucked a branch free, taking a whole week at once.

His attacker barely flinched.

Reed writhed against the wall, panic surging through his limbs as he snatched another branch, and then a third. *What the fuck?* Treveyon's grip remained as iron; the man seemed possessed of rage, utterly blind to the way his life was being stolen. Reed sunk his fingers – now as bones – into the man's flesh and clawed at yet more branches, harvesting *years* with each swipe now and still Treveyon did not yield – his eyes blazed with madness, a lust to kill.

More white leaves went flying.

On and on Reed tore at the tree, even as his vision grew black and only the white trunk remained. Yet somehow he clung to life, something just as animalistic within him roared back as it ripped the entire trunk free in a spray of earth – and suddenly he had all the time in the world.

Reed held the trunk in his hands, ragged branches empty or snapped at one end, and at the other – blackened roots writhing, as if screaming in a silent cacophony.

He brought the trunk crashing down across his knee.

It snapped clean in half, splinting into a million shimmering fragments.

Reed hit the floor.

He blinked against a white avalanche that followed, gasping in sweet air, or so he hoped, but he could not hold on...

***

Reed woke in a wide room of bright marble floors and walls; they stretched endlessly no matter where he turned. Fluted columns stood evenly spaced, patterned in interlocking squares, rectangles and even triangles – but so, so very densely. No archways were visible and the marble did not end with the structure; thousands, possibly millions of stools and tables had been arranged in lines of vertigo-inducing rigidness, perfectly aligned chess sets sitting atop the smooth surfaces.

And waiting at each table; the same elderly man in a yellow and white robe.

His beard reached down to a thick leather belt and

his head bore wild tufts of white hair, as if it had grown independently of each other in both time and space. The man played against invisible opponents all, speaking often, moving pieces, waving his hands as if to no-one, but Reed did not doubt that there were other players.

"Reed."

He blinked.

The same old man now sat across from him, hands folded before his half of the set – white, while the black pieces waited before Reed.

Jupiter.

Father of all Gods – mighty arbitrator and creator, a figure none dared cross.

"Lord Jupiter," Reed replied. He swallowed – he'd never come close to meeting even a *servant* of Jupiter, let alone the great god himself.

The old man sighed as he regarded Reed, and somewhere below, thunder echoed. His eyes were a deep black without irises and the longer Reed looked into them, the more the black seemed to be pulling him in, closer and smaller, of less and less significance, tiny of thought and deed; he was merely half-human, merely half-Reaper. He was merely *existing* – nothing he could ever do, think or achieve would impact Jupiter or his design... and yet, there was no shame in the sensation. Instead, relief and acceptance; it was entirely acceptable to use only the power that he held and to work within his own sphere, to be smaller but to understand that smaller was not the same as 'less'.

"You have broken quite a few rules lately, my boy."

Reed blinked. *What the hell was all that? It was like... like he was reducing me down, squashing my mind, my sense of self*

– only to rebuild me?

The great god was waiting.

"I have." No point lying or offering an explanation.

Jupiter nodded. "The business with that poor ghost Lily comes to mind. Further to that, you have promised her much that is beyond your ability to grant – a cruel thing to do, don't you think? There is also the matter of what you have promised young Sol, yes? A second instance where your Word has been given in a situation where you may not be able to deliver upon it."

"Yes," Reed replied. He swallowed – was he still to be punished? And what was he going to face? Death? Vanishing? Obliteration? Limbo? There was no precedent to draw on. *Anything* could happen – not just the usual things limited to the Underworld or other realms of death; that was just his fear trying to assign control via expectation of consequences. *Shit, shit, shit.*

"And your final indiscretion is what I like to call the Big One. Even the fruit of Mors cannot be given exceptions. You are well aware of this."

"I am."

The old man sat back, linking his hands behind his head in a pose that was extremely un-godlike. "Well then, what do you have to say, son?"

Reed closed his eyes a moment. What to say? Nothing could save him. He just had to... speak. Reed opened his eyes – Jupiter regarded him with a look of infinite patience. "Can you tell me; are my cousins safe from the Shining Leaves now?"

Jupiter regarded Reed a long moment before a faint smile crossed his pale lips. The black of his eyes grew mirror-like, rather than the dense vacuums of before. "They are indeed."

Reed slumped a little on his own stool. "Good."

"Very well, a fine enough question. Let me try another – what consequences do you believe you ought to face?"

"I would like to start by forfeiting the time I took from Treveyon."

A nod. "It has already been done."

"I want to keep my promises."

Again, Jupiter nodded. "That is something I also expect – and I also suspect you know that doing so will represent some penance in and of itself."

"And I want to help stop Feronia's decay."

"Ah, now things grow interesting, for some would argue that such a task would be an even greater punishment."

"I have doubtless earned it."

"Perhaps, perhaps not. Let me show you what happened when Mors closed the Fringe." Jupiter tapped the chess board and it spun aside with a grinding, revealing a clear, still pool of water where the table ought to have rested. "Look within."

Reed did and frowned at the image that resolved – Feronia's green hideaway, swarming with figures. Many were Reapers: his cousins, though they'd been joined by men and women in hunter's garb, including Adrina, and also warlike folk belonging to Mars as they fought the vine and tentacle beast that was the unfinished Feronia.

Both his cousins and those that were far more distant relatives hacked and slashed at the Goddess with scythes, sickles, swords and axes. With each blow green spewed forth and where it landed, grass, flowers and fruit bloomed...

only to quickly turn to rot.

And though the combatants were smashed aside or sent flying out of view, they always returned to resume their task until Feronia began to shrink, her as-yet-unformed body soon rendered a motionless pile of mulch, and then the children stopped at last, leaning upon their weapons to catch their breath.

"Did you see it?"

Reed glanced back at the Father. "What did I miss?"

"Nearest that most enthusiastic child of Mars, what do you see by his sandal?"

Once again, Reed watched the battle – and flinched back when he caught what Jupiter had noticed. The mighty axe of Mars' servant cut through one of Feronia's many wrists, severing a hand. The moment it hit the ground, the hand scrambled away like a gangly green spider.

"And now that it is loose I can see a grim future for humanity if such a thing is allowed to spread its decay."

"We'll be overrun?"

"It is possible. But more troubling; I cannot see Feronia's hand any longer. Something is intervening."

Reed gaped. "Something can actually do that?"

Jupiter chuckled. "There are several things out there that might trouble even Gods such as I."

Reed shivered.

"And so let us return to your penance. You will assist my children in discovering what or who is behind the disappearance of Feronia's hand."

"I fear my might is paltry but you have it."

"Do not fear, there are many tasks which must be completed and some of them must be done in your plane and so you are certainly going to be useful.'

"Thank you."

The old god lifted a pawn then, meeting Reed's gaze. In the dark mirrors, Reed caught his own expression – one of returning fear. "And no more breaking the Big Rule, Reed, for next time I may not have need of you, and if that is the case, what transpires after will not be to your liking."

Chapter 27.

Reed woke to screeching of a bandsaw.

Screw you, Steve.

But at least what he saw above was his roof, the softness below was from his bed. A tiny pair of blessings perhaps, but welcome ones.

He rose to sit in a patch of pale, emaciated sunlight that fell across the rumpled blanket. The rest of the room was too dim to see much. He swallowed and winced, throat still tender. He found a glass of old water and took a drink, but even that hurt, then stumbled to the ensuite where he frowned into the mirror – not at his unruly hair nor stubble, but the red marks that covered his neck.

"You actually look a little better than yesterday."

Reed glanced over his shoulder. Lina stood in the doorway, her expression sombre. "Did you get me out of SEDO's office?"

She nodded. "Max too. We took care of Treveyon's body but your detective friend is going to have some questions when he finds out – we had to sedate the two cult members."

"I'll handle the police," he said. *Somehow.* "Thanks, Lina."

"There's something else."

He ran the tap and splashed water across his face, the cold banishing any remnants of sleep. "Feronia's hand? Jupiter himself told me about it right before he put me on the case and promised... bad things if I broke the rules again."

She sighed. "That was a nasty surprise."

"He thinks something's actually managed to hide the hand," Reed replied as he dried his face with a hand towel. He leant against the bench and Lina's jaw was clenched. "What the fuck could hide from Jupiter, right?"

"That's what we have to find out."

"How?"

"Mother suggested a visit to Minerva."

That made sense – who better than the Goddess of Wisdom? "But she's not going herself?"

"I didn't want to argue with her, you know what she's like – she prefers to stick to her role."

"Yeah, but she'll send us into the fray, right?"

Lina shrugged. "I want to do this."

Reed started for the kitchen and Lina followed, watching him pour milk into a tall glass. Chewing probably wasn't the best idea today anyway, not with his throat the way it was. "There's something I have to do before that – I need to find Elise's killer." *And figure out what happened to Mum and Dad... after Elise. She's finally going to be put first.*

"Then you need to find Dunstall, right? He's the next lead."

"I have a few more options but I think you're right." There was still the casino and Jordan from SEDO too. It was possible that Veronica and the Shining Leaves had tried to recruit Elise before or after she tried to back out of the role of dealer or mule… though killing a prospective member of a cult seemed excessive, unless the girl saw something? It wasn't all adding up yet, that much was clear. *Another reason your work isn't done there.*

"Well, don't give up," Lina said with a smile. "You're pretty good at this stuff, you know."

"Thanks, Cousin."

"Now, about that other thing I mentioned. I got a visit from one of Pluto's grubs; he's looking for you."

Reed straightened. How could he have forgotten? "The spirit-worm. Shit."

"Yes. The grub told me to let you know that most of it suddenly dissolved; they're following the remains but it left something behind."

"What?"

Lina reached into her robe and withdrew what seemed to be a knucklebone, which she placed on the table. She hesitated. "Ready?"

"Lina, what's this about?"

"The grub said that this belonged to your father, Reed."

Epilogue

There were no more traces of Reed's father beneath the city.

At least, none Reed could find.

The stone floor of the massive drain was rich with decades of water stains and other debris, only faintly illuminated by his torch. But where was once a mass of red and black, the worm-like bundle of dark emotions, had writhed as it lay being devoured by Pluto's grubs, now only shadows remained beneath St Paul's cathedral.

"I told you we wouldn't find anything," Lina said. She stood before a mirror image of herself, checking her hair, though she glanced at him and there was some concern in her eyes.

Reed shook his head. "Fine, but I had to come here anyway."

"I know."

"What else did the grub say?" Reed asked.

"Not much, just what I said before – he told me to give you the knuckle bone and that it was your father's. Maybe it's a trap?"

"Set by who?"

"No idea."

"Few would be able to put Pluto's servants up to something like that. And if it *is* a trap, why haven't they sprung it yet? We've been down here for a while."

"True enough. So, what now?"

Reed kicked at a clump of muck. "Search the cathedral I suppose."

"You think one of the priests stole your father's bones?"

"Not really." After all, that would imply that complete strangers actually knew where his father's body rested. And more, it assumed there was a body at rest. According to Aunty, no-one knew that for sure. *If she's actually been telling the truth all these years.* "Lina, can you call your mother?"

She sniffed. "Do it yourself."

"I don't have a coin – and besides, she'll come quicker if you do it."

"Fine," she said with a sigh. "Mother, Reed wants to talk."

Mors shimmered into view before them, resplendent in inky robes, her shawl whispering as her skull turned to regard him. "Reed."

"One of Pluto's grubs found a knuckle bone that belonged to my father."

"That I know. Did you call me here to tell me such a thing?"

"No. I want to know what's going on."

Death lifted a smooth hand; her nails tipped in black, and snapped her fingers. A wavering image appeared before them – that of a black lake still as glass. A tall throne rose up from the centre, this white monster slender and sharp.

Sitting upon it was a man of cobalt-blue, pale eyes luminous – even his teeth were aglow when he spoke.

"Mors? How can I help you and your children..." He squinted. "Lina is it? And Reed Lavender too; I have not seen either of you in some time. You must visit more often."

"Reed is searching for his father," Mors said.

"Again?"

Reed lifted the knucklebone. "This was found after a 'spirit-worm' was dissolved."

"I know it, Reed."

"Then do you know what it means?"

Pluto shrugged from his throne, crossing his legs at the ankles. He wore lace-up boots polished to a high sheen. "It is as I said all those years ago – your father and mother have Vanished, yet they are not wholly gone. Your aunt and I have already searched long and wide."

"As have you yourself," Mors added to Reed.

"And all any of us ever found out was that they aren't *here* anymore," Reed said. "So isn't this a clue? And a better one than those symbols?"

"If it is, find the source of the spirit-worm and you will find another clue, surely?" Pluto replied. His voice still boomed, leaping across the lake to fill the drain. Grains of sand or dirt were shaken loose.

"Your servants found nothing?"

"Its source was not localised to the cathedral, only that it gathered there," Pluto replied. "As ever, such... weaknesses excrete from humans at all times in all places."

Lina giggled, presumably at the description.

"Then if you haven't investigated already, I will."

"Please," Pluto replied. "Until we speak again. Sister."

"Brother." The image disappeared. Mors turned to regard him with her fathomless eye-sockets. "Are you satisfied?"

"Not yet, but thank you."

"Then I will return to my duties – be sure you do not neglect yours, Reed. We both know just how many debts you must now fill. I expect you to maintain the family honour."

"Of course."

"Lina? Enough playing with your cousin."

Lina shrugged. "Bye Reed."

Both disappeared and Reed exhaled, long and slow. He put his father's knucklebone back into his pocket and started toward the surface and home, his footfalls echoing in the dark.

A Note from Ashley

Greetings! I hope you enjoyed Graves Robbed, Heirlooms Returned and thanks for reading.

I'd like to ask if you could help me out by leaving an honest review of the book at your place of purchase? Long or short, bad or good, it all helps!

AND if you'd like to sign up to my newsletter you'll be the first to know when the next Reed Lavender story is released. You'll also have first access to preview chapters and pre-release editions of the story, in addition to being automatically added into the draw for giveaways.

Ashley

ACKNOWLEDGMENTS

Firstly, I want to thank my wife Brooke for her constant support and belief in me!

Also, to everyone who works hard to help me at every stage of the process, but especially Rebekah at VividCovers for yet another great cover.

Ashley Capes